"Thank you."

Jonah turned and found Mallory standing on the bottom step, her fingers touching the wooden handrail. "For reading to him. You made his night. He was worried about sleeping away from the ranch tonight. Worried my parents wouldn't be able to sleep without him being there."

A smile tugged at her lips as she lowered her gaze.

He moved toward her. "He's such a great kid, Mal. You're an amazing mom. Thank you for opening the door for me. I know I don't deserve it. I'm just going to keep proving I've changed so I don't have to walk back out it again. Someday."

Mallory held up a hand. "One day at a time. Okay? Keep showing up for Tanner, and we'll see how the rest goes."

He shoved his hands into his pockets again and nodded.

He'd definitely keep showing up. He'd be the kind of dad his son deserved. And prove his worth to Mallory—whatever it took.

Heart, home and faith have always been important to **Lisa Jordan**, so writing stories with those elements comes naturally. Happily married for over thirty years to her real-life hero, she and her husband have two grown sons and two rascal rescue dogs. In her free time, Lisa enjoys quality family time, reading and being creative with friends. Learn more about her by visiting www.lisajordanbooks.com.

Books by Lisa Jordan

Love Inspired

Lakeside Reunion
Lakeside Family
Lakeside Sweethearts
Lakeside Redemption
Lakeside Romance
Season of Hope
A Love Redeemed
The Father He Deserves
His Road to Redemption

Stone River Ranch

Rescuing Her Ranch
Redeeming the Cowboy
Bonding with the Cowboy's Daughter

K-9 Companions

Earning the Veteran's Trust

Visit the Author Profile page at LoveInspired.com.

EARNING THE VETERAN'S TRUST

LISA JORDAN

LOVE INSPIRED
INSPIRATIONAL ROMANCE

LOVE INSPIRED®
INSPIRATIONAL ROMANCE

Recycling programs
for this product may
not exist in your area.

ISBN-13: 978-1-335-93189-4

Earning the Veteran's Trust

Copyright © 2025 by Lisa Jordan

Love Inspired
22 Adelaide St. West, 41st Floor
Toronto, Ontario M5H 4E3, Canada
www.LoveInspired.com

Printed in Lithuania

MIX
Paper | Supporting
responsible forestry
FSC® C021394

But now thus saith the Lord that created thee,
O Jacob, and he that formed thee, O Israel,
Fear not: for I have redeemed thee, I have called thee
by thy name; thou art mine.
—*Isaiah* 43:1

To Darla and Brett Miller, whose love for rescuing senior and disabled animals inspired this story.

Acknowledgments

Lord, may my words glorify You.

My family—Patrick, Scott and Mitchell.
You are the best. I love you forever.

Thanks to Matthew McClellan and Kathy Copen
for answering my research questions.
Any mistakes are mine.

Thanks to Jeanne Takenaka, Alena Tauriainen,
Wendy Galinetti, Heidi McCahan and Linda Jo Reed
for your prayers, brainstorming,
encouragement and sprinting.

Thanks to Cynthia Ruchti, my awesome agent,
and Melissa Endlich, my exceptional editor,
for your support, grace and patience.
Thanks to the Love Inspired team who work hard
to bring my books to print.

Chapter One

Mallory Stone hadn't expected to spend her birthday looking for a new place to live.

It was time to move off her family's cattle ranch in Aspen Ridge, Colorado, and find a home where she could raise her seven-year-old son.

Her online search for housing had been disappointing, and it would need to wait for now.

Her best friend needed her.

Mallory drove down the winding tree-lined drive that led to the Wallen Fruit Farm adjacent to her family's ranch and parked her silver Subaru behind her friend's Jeep.

Leaving the warmth of her heated seats, she stepped out into the early-April air. A chilly breeze brushed across her cheeks.

She shut off the engine and pocketed her keys, then reached for a cardboard carrier with two steaming cups of chai latte from her aunt's diner and a box with two decadent brownies guaranteed to wash away any negative emotions. She set them on the roof of her car, then opened the back door and unclipped the canine seat belt from Rosie's harness. She reached for the leash. "Come on, girl. Let's go comfort Bri."

Her nine-year-old buff-colored cocker spaniel jumped down and waited at Mallory's side while she closed the door and retrieved the coffee and brownies.

Threading the leash over her hand, Mallory headed up the cobblestone walk lined with colorful flowers waving in the midmorning breeze and then stepped onto the gray farmhouse porch. She rang the doorbell. Barking followed by fast footsteps sounded seconds before the door was yanked open.

Brianna Wallen-Jewell—or Bri, as Mallory had called her best friend since second grade—stood in the doorway with her strawberry-blond hair pulled back in a messy ponytail. Her red-rimmed eyes matched the oversize pink sweatshirt she wore over black leggings. She wadded a tissue in her hand.

Seeing Mallory, she flung her arms around her and sobbed against Mallory's neck.

Leo, Bri's black-and-tan Yorkie, danced around their feet, but Rosie remained quiet at Mallory's side.

Mallory tried to juggle the drink carrier and bakery box while offering sympathy and preventing getting tangled in Rosie's leash. "Hey, what's all this about?"

Bri pulled back and crushed the wadded-up tissue to her eyes. "My marriage is over."

"What? You and Cam are perfect for each other." Even though her friend had a flair for the dramatic, the words and the tears appeared to be very real.

Fresh tears streamed down Bri's face as she turned and ushered Mallory and Rosie into the farmhouse that had been in her family for three generations. Leo trailed after them.

Mallory edged the door closed with her foot, then followed her friend into the kitchen. Morning light streamed through the sheer curtains, spilling sunshine across the floor, as she set the drinks and box on the retro red Formica and stainless steel table sitting next to the large window. After she unclipped Rosie's leash and hung it over the back of the chair, the dog settled on the floor at Mallory's feet.

Leo raced back into the living room, his nails tapping against the aged hardwood floors.

Bri pulled out a matching vinyl chair and buried her face in her folded arms.

Mallory removed her friend's favorite brew from the cardboard carrier and pushed it toward her. "Drink this and tell me what happened."

Bri lifted her head and braced her elbow on the table. Cupping her face with her hand, she reached for the to-go cup. "It's this stupid farm, that's what happened."

"You love this place."

"Sure, when my grandparents ran it. Then while Mom and Dad took it over after Grandpa died. But since Cam and I got married and took it over, it's been a lot of work to make a go of the place while still holding down full-time jobs. And Cam's dad just offered him a promotion in his cybersecurity firm, which would mean moving to Durango instead of working remotely, as he'd been doing. Cam suggested selling the farm, which led to a fight. He said I had to choose between him or the farm."

"And you chose the farm?" Mallory leaned back in her chair and sipped her chai latte. "I find that hard to believe."

Bri dragged her fingers through her hair, dislodging it from the ponytail. "He didn't give me time to answer. He took his laptop and left. I've been a mess since he stormed out of the house an hour ago."

Mallory stood and moved to the sink. She wet a paper towel under warm water and handed it to Bri. "Here—wash your face. Cam loves you. He's not leaving you without an explanation or discussing this. What do you want to do?"

"I want to build a life with my husband. Have a family someday. We've been married for four years, but we've been too busy to think about having children. I'm so tired of being tired. I'm sorry to dump all of this in your lap." Bri covered her face with the damp paper towel.

"Hey, what are friends for? What can I do to help?"

Bri let out a deep sigh, dropped the paper towel on the table and looked at Mallory. "Cam always wanted to follow in his dad's footsteps. Now that the vice president position has been offered, he wants to take the job."

"What about your job? Have you talked to Jacie yet?"

"I haven't had time. His dad's offer came in last night. Today's my day off from the bridal shop, but if Cam and I can have a reasonable conversation about this, then I will give her my notice tomorrow. I just hate the idea of the farm leaving my family." She reached for her latte, took a sip and then lifted her eyes back to Mallory. "Would you consider staying here for a while and overseeing the place while Cam and I decide what we're doing with our future?"

Mallory didn't believe in coincidences. Was the Lord answering her prayer already after this morning's dismal house-hunting search?

"You mean like house-sitting?" Mallory returned to her chair across from Bri. "Staying here short-term would give me time to find a permanent home. But I do have Tanner to consider. He loves the ranch, but I would like my own space."

Bri stood and moved to the sink. "Forget it. It's a bad idea. I shouldn't have asked."

"Hey, now. Give me a minute to process. How long are you talking?"

"I don't know yet. When Cam asked if I'd consider selling the farm, I countered with getting away for a bit and see if we'd miss it."

"So, you're seriously thinking of selling?"

Bri shrugged. "I don't know. Maybe." She laughed. "Want to buy a farm?"

Mallory returned to the sink and looked out the window. Rows of apple trees with green buds cast skeletal shadows across the recently planted strawberry patch.

Mallory didn't like making decisions on the spot, preferring to weigh out her options. The timing of Bri's offer, though...

"I have wonderful childhood memories of this place. Picking strawberries and apples with my mom and grandma. And your grandparents' strawberry festivals were the best." Mallory turned to her friend. "My family nearly lost the ranch a couple of years ago, so I get why you want to hold on to the farm. I'm not family, but I'll try it."

Bri's eyes lit up. "You'll house-sit?"

"Yes, on two conditions." Mallory held up two fingers.

Bri clasped her hands in front of her and grinned. "Anything. You name it."

"One, if it's too much, then I can move back to the ranch with no hard feelings between us. And two, if you do decide to sell, then I have first option."

Bri's jaw dropped. "Seriously? Why would you want this place when you have your parents' gorgeous ranch?"

"The ranch belongs to my parents. I want my own space. And room for Tanner to run."

"But you can find a house with a yard. Why would you want a forty-acre farm? It's a lot of work."

"I've been looking for something with some acreage to buy so I have space to rescue dogs—particularly seniors, so they don't have to spend their remaining years in shelters."

"Didn't you do a service project in high school on adopting rescue dogs?"

Mallory nodded. "So many families want cute puppies. Older dogs are harder to place. Since I've taken over the administrative work at the animal shelter, I've seen some of the same dogs remain unadopted for months. With my siblings' families growing and the dogs all over the place at the ranch, I don't see Mom and Dad being too thrilled if I adopt a few. But with my own place…" She lifted a shoulder. "Maybe I could pair them with people needing comfort as they work through their own forms of trauma."

"Oh, girl. If anyone can do it, you and your

big heart can help them. Sadly, since you've had your own fair share." Bri threw her arms around Mallory's neck. "Wait until I tell Cam. He'll be thrilled. Just knowing we have a house sitter will help us make some plans. Thank you, Mal. You're the best friend a girl could ask for."

She returned the hug, then smothered an unexpected yawn.

Bri stepped back and eyed Mallory. "You're not sleeping well again. The nightmares are back?"

"Not 'back,' exactly. Last night, I watched a movie with Mom, Dad and Everly that had a hostage situation. It triggered another nightmare. Thankfully, I didn't call out, but Everly complained about my restlessness keeping her up. We haven't shared a room since we were teenagers. Since leaving the navy last August, I've invaded her turf. This morning, my counselor suggested stepping out of my comfort zone and start looking for a new place. So that's what I was doing until you texted, asking me to come over."

Hazy images of last night's dream tugged at memories she tried to keep tucked away. No matter how much she tried, she'd never forget the feeling of the cold muzzle of the Beretta pressed against her temple. Or the hot breath of the angry sailor with his arm constricting her throat. She balled her fists as her chest tightened.

Rosie pawed at her leg, jerking Mallory from the past. She crouched and wrapped her arms around the cocker spaniel. The canine comfort was enough to return her rapid heartbeat to its regular rhythm.

Her phone chimed. She pulled it out of her back pocket and found a text from her mom, reminding Mallory of their lunch date. She stood. "Sorry to cut this short, but I'm meeting Mom for lunch, then we're getting pedicures. Want to join us?"

"Thanks, but I'm a mess. I need to shower and text Cam. Maybe there's hope for my marriage after all." Shaking her head, Bri tugged on the hem of her T-shirt. Then she looked at Mallory with wide eyes as she covered her mouth. "Today's your birthday, and I made it all about me. I'm so sorry! I have a gift for you. It's on the coffee table."

Bri linked her arm through Mallory's and pulled her toward the living room. She reached for a lavender gift bag and handed it to Mallory. Leo jumped up on the royal blue couch and burrowed next to a bright orange throw pillow.

Rosie sat at Mallory's feet as she pulled out a soft hand-knitted scarf in shades of blue and wound it around her neck. "Bri! This is gorgeous. Thank you."

Bri shrugged. "I was sorting through my grandma's totes of yarn and found that skein. It reminded me of you right away. I know it's spring, but you can always save it for next year."

"We're in Colorado. It's not unheard of to have snow in June." She brushed the soft fibers against her cheek. "It's perfect. I love it. Thank you."

Heavy footsteps sounded on the porch. Leo jumped off the couch and shot to the door, barking as it flew open.

"Bri! Baby! Pack your bags. I found the solution to our problems. Jonah offered to buy the farm." Cameron Jewell—or Cam, as his family and friends called him—sauntered into the house. His dark blond hair was tousled by the midmorning breeze and his bright blue eyes shone.

But Mallory's focus gravitated from her best friend's husband to the man who followed him inside.

The same man who had been tiptoeing in and out of her dreams for the past eight years.

Jonah Hayes.

The air wheezed from her lungs as her mouth dried.

If only she hadn't given her word to house-sit only moments ago.

Because at that very second, Mallory wanted nothing more than to grab her son and escape the state of Colorado.

Or maybe even the country.

She'd go any place to get away from the man looking at her with wide eyes. The man who'd promised her everything, then left her with nothing but a broken heart. The man who'd denied his own son.

Now it was her turn to walk away, but her feet wouldn't move.

"Mallory." Her name fell from his mouth in an incredulous whisper. "What are you doing here?"

Bri frowned. "You two know each other?"

Tightening her fingers around the strings on the gift bag, Mallory swallowed several times, crossed her arms over her chest and found her voice. She looked at Jonah. "I could ask you the same thing, but I really don't care."

"Wait a minute." Cam stepped between them. "Mal, how do you know my cousin?"

Mallory's eyes shot to his face. "Cousin? Jonah's your cousin?"

"Yeah, his mom is my dad's younger sister."

Mallory let out a laugh that sounded more like a cough and a wheeze. "This is getting even better. My best friend is related to the last man I ever wanted to see again."

"Last man?" Frowning, Bri touched her arm. "Mal, what's going on?"

Mallory shook her head.

What could she say? Really? She hadn't shared her most humiliating secret with anyone. Not even her family.

But the truth was going to come out, especially if they were in the same town.

Arms folded over her chest, Mallory lifted her chin and glared at Jonah. "He's my ex-husband."

Bri's chin dropped. Hurt flashed in her green eyes. "You two got married, and you didn't tell me?" She turned to Cam. "Did you know?"

He frowned. "Of course not. I wouldn't keep something like that from you."

"About that..." Jonah cleared his throat and took a step toward her, but Rosie moved between them. "Mallory, can I have a minute?"

Feeling like she had a noose around her neck, Mallory unwound the scarf her friend had given her and curled her fingers in the fibers. "For what?"

"I need to talk to you."

"We have nothing to say."

He scrubbed a hand over his face. "You're going to want to hear this. Please."

Bri laid a hand on Mallory's shoulder. "Couldn't hurt to hear him out, Mal."

Easy for her to say.

She exhaled and stuffed the scarf back into the gift bag. "Fine. What?"

Jonah shifted his eyes from her to Bri and Cam. Bri grabbed Cam's hand and headed toward the kitchen. She paused in front of Jonah. "Hurt her and you deal with me."

He nodded. "Noted."

After they left, Jonah shoved a hand in his pocket and ran another over his military-short hair. "So, uh, the thing is, I'm not your ex-husband."

A chill crawled across her skin. "What are you talking about?"

"We're still married." He looked at her with serious eyes, but this had to be some sort of sick joke.

Had to be.

"We're what?" Mallory blinked, her voice barely a whisper. The three words created a sickening feeling in her stomach.

"Still married."

"How is that even possible? I signed the papers. Mailed them back." Her tone rose with each word. She scanned her memory. She'd received a divorce decree…didn't she?

She'd gotten so sidetracked with terrible bouts of morning sickness and then raising her child on her own that she'd forgotten about the paperwork that dissolved her brief marriage.

As Rosie leaned against Mallory, she rested a hand on the dog's head. She pressed the other one against her chest as her breathing constricted.

Jonah rushed over to her. "Hey, are you okay? You went white."

Rosie moved in front of Mallory again, blocking Jonah from approaching her.

Jonah stepped back and put his hands up.

Mallory glared at him. "Of course I went

white. You show up out of the blue and drop this bomb on me. What'd you expect?"

He flinched. "I'm sorry."

"You're sorry? Where was that apology eight years ago?" Shaking her head, Mallory strode into the kitchen and grabbed her purse and Rosie's leash off the back of the chair, refusing to make eye contact with Cam and Bri, who must've heard every word, and returned to the living room.

She clipped the leash to Rosie's harness, then walked backward toward the door. "I can't do this."

With tears blurring her vision, she rushed out the front door.

That was not how she expected to spend her birthday. And, as much as it pained her to do it, Mallory had to go back on her word to her friend. Because there was no way she could stay in Aspen Ridge. Not with Jonah back in town.

This time, she had more than her heart to lose.

Never in a million years did Jonah Hayes expect to see his wife standing in his cousin's living room.

Now that he'd come face-to-face with the one person he'd hurt the most, somehow he needed to show Mallory he wasn't the same guy she'd married nearly eight years ago.

After all, redemption had a cost, and Jonah was

willing to pay whatever price was necessary to restore his marriage.

The marriage he didn't deserve but desperately wanted.

He hurried after her, the front door slamming behind him. "Mallory, wait!"

With her long, dark hair hanging sleek and straight to the middle of her back, Mallory paused midway up the walk, turned and stared at him with those brown eyes that showed nothing of the love she'd once claimed to have had for him.

Love he destroyed because he allowed fear to ruin the best thing that had happened to him.

"I signed the papers, Jonah. And mailed them to you." Her words, spoken low but with precision, spiked him in the chest.

"Yeah, I know. I just didn't get them submitted in the ninety-day window, so technically, we're still married."

Mallory shook her head. "Why didn't my lawyer say something? Why'd you wait nearly eight years to tell me, for that matter?"

"I've been busy, okay?" He kicked his toe against the cobblestone walk.

"No, it's not okay. What if I'd met someone and got married in that time? I would've committed bigamy without knowing it."

His head shot up. "Did you? Get married again?"

She scoffed. "Are you kidding? I learned my

lesson the first time. If you couldn't stand being married to me for less than a month, why would I give some other guy a chance to ditch me? Other than my dad and brothers, men can't be trusted."

He took a step toward her. "Mallory…"

Once again, her dog moved in front of her. Mallory threw a hand up faster than a traffic cop. "Don't. This is your mess. You need to fix it. Submit the original papers, and we can go our separate ways."

He swallowed hard. "I can't."

"Why not?"

"I don't know where they are."

"Jonah…" She turned away, shaking her head.

She didn't have to say it. Her disappointment was written all over her face.

"Even if I could, I don't want to."

Her eyes narrowed. "You don't want to what?"

"End our marriage."

Her jaw dropped open, but nothing came out. She closed it again, shook her head and gripped her dog's leash. "Jonah, you were right—our marriage was a mistake. Let's end it and get on with our lives."

"But I was wrong. Our marriage wasn't a mistake. I shouldn't have said that. I'm the one who made the mistake. I returned to Colorado to make amends with my family. Then, I planned to get in touch with your brother, Bear, to get your address so I could talk to you. A lot has happened in the last eight years. I'm not the same man you married. Give me a chance to prove it."

She stepped back. "Prove it? If you wanted to do that, then why did it take you this long to come back?"

Jonah dragged a hand over his face. He so did not want to play the sympathy card, but he was done with keeping secrets. "I was severely injured the same day I received your papers and spent the next several years learning how to walk again. I went down a dark path, then ended up on a farm in Pennsylvania that gave me a new lease on life."

Jonah lifted his head and found Mallory blinking rapidly as her eyes shimmered. She bit her bottom lip. "I'm sorry to hear that. I didn't know."

"No one did. I wouldn't allow them to contact Dad or anyone else. I was ashamed. The last thing I wanted to be was someone else's burden."

He'd let that wrong thinking keep him from getting in touch with people he'd hurt. Until he finally realized that they were being hurt more by his silence, his absence. Just as he'd hurt the woman standing in front of him. He wished he could tell her all this and more, but he didn't want her pity, didn't want her giving him another chance because she felt sorry for him. He wanted a fresh start because she still had feelings for him, but it was quite clear any love she had for him was gone.

Mallory took a step toward him and pressed a hand against his arm. His heart jumped to his throat. "No one would have thought that."

The sincerity in her voice untangled the knot in his gut. "Yeah, I get that now. Once I sought counseling in Pennsylvania, I reached out to Dad and Cam. I wanted to return to Aspen Ridge when I could make my family proud."

And that included the woman standing before him.

"Cam and I reunited a few weeks ago. We had breakfast this morning, and he told me about his dad's offer as well as the problems with the farm. We're both only children, so we grew up more like brothers. I wanted to make up for the years I'd lost with him, so I offered to buy the farm so he could pursue his career without being weighed down by other obligations. That way, Bri's farm could still stay in the family. Sort of."

"That's very noble of you." The words didn't sound like a compliment, and Mallory winced. "Sorry. I do mean it—that *was* a kind offer. Problem is, you're not the only one who wants to buy the farm."

Jonah frowned. "Cam didn't mention it being on the market, let alone having another party interested."

"That's because she just learned about the potential sale." Mallory looked away.

"She?" He scowled, then realized what she'd meant. "You? You want to buy the farm?"

She lifted a shoulder. "Sure, why not?"

"What would you do with it? Forty acres is a bit much for one person to manage."

"But it's okay for you to buy it?"

"I wouldn't be going at it alone. If I do buy the farm, I plan to create an accessible garden to help disabled vets like me grow their own produce."

"Like a community garden?"

He shrugged. "Maybe. Cam and I talked about starting a CSA project—a community supported agriculture project where people could support the farm and get a stake of the produce." He lifted his chin. "What would you do with so much land?"

She turned her back to him. "I'd adopt senior dogs to give them space to spend their final years in freedom, not locked in a shelter where they'd been abandoned."

Abandoned.

The word rippled through him.

What he'd done to her.

But not this time. He wouldn't turn his back on her again.

Her anger was quite apparent, and he didn't blame her. She had every right after what he'd done. But the farm could offer more than a chance to use his new skills for others—maybe just maybe he could show Mallory he was a new man and deeply sorry for what he'd put her through.

He took another step toward her, reached for her arm and turned her to face him. "Let's buy the farm. Together. You can rescue all the dogs you want, and I'll use part of the property for adaptive gardening and start the CSA project."

She glanced at his hand but didn't shrug it off. "It's not that simple."

He exhaled. "I don't expect you to trust me just because I say I've changed. Give me a chance to show you."

Mallory dropped her chin to her chest and shook her head. Then she raised her head again and looked at him directly. "This isn't just about me. Or you. There's more to it than that."

"Whatever it is, we'll make it work."

"Jonah, I have a son." The words came out in a rush. She swallowed and looked away. "Actually, *we* have a son."

The air whooshed out of his lungs as fire spread through him. His ears buzzed as those two words swirled in his head.

A son.

He opened his mouth, and this time, he was the one lacking words. He shook his head to stop the humming in his ears.

"We have a son?" The words wheezed from

his chest. "When? We were together for only a short time before I deployed."

"We eloped and had a three-day honeymoon at that cute cottage in Virginia Beach, remember?"

No matter how many knocks he'd taken to the head, he would never forget the vows he'd made on the beach to the most beautiful woman on the planet.

"A couple of weeks after sending back the papers, I learned I was pregnant. I emailed and sent a letter, asking you to contact me. When you didn't, I figured you didn't want to hear from me."

His vision blurred as his throat thickened. "I'm sorry, Mal. So sorry. For so many things. It wasn't a matter of wanting…"

A thousand thoughts raced through his mind. His remorse over divorcing her and for not reaching out sooner now snowballed into a huge mountain of regret. He'd wasted precious time when he could have been getting to know his son. He had to sort out how to deal with those feelings, but now, he had new responsibilities.

No more excuses. It was time to man up and face his actions.

He straightened his shoulders, dragged a finger and thumb over his damp eyes, and cleared his throat. "My offer stands—let's be the family we're supposed to be." He waved a hand over the property. "We can raise our son together here."

She shook her head. "No way. He doesn't even know you."

"We can change that. It will be a fresh start for all of us."

"For you, you mean. You don't even know me anymore. You don't know what I've been through. You don't even know my son's name."

"*Our* son."

"Until three minutes ago, you didn't know he existed."

"You're right. I'm sorry. I want to make it right. Give me a chance to start over."

"I can't do this right now." She turned away from him, yanked her keys out of her pocket and headed for her car.

"Hey, Mal?"

She stopped but didn't turn. "What?"

"Happy birthday."

She paused, but without saying anything, she opened her rear door and stepped back while her dog jumped inside.

This time, Jonah didn't go after her. But he wasn't about to let this be the end of the discussion. He'd give her a little time, then he'd approach her again. He'd prove he was the right man for her and the best dad for... She was right—he didn't even know their son's name.

He'd learn it and so much more. Whatever it took because he wasn't about to walk away from his family again. Second chances didn't come along every day, so he was about to make the most of the one he was given.

If only Mallory would give him another opportunity to prove he wasn't the man he used to be.

Chapter Two

No way could Mallory make a life with Jonah again after he'd betrayed her once already. Not when she couldn't trust him to stay.

So why couldn't she get their earlier conversation out of her head as she scraped the dinner plates and loaded them into the dishwasher?

Laughter floated through the open kitchen window of her parents' ranch house. Mallory pulled back the curtain in time to see Tanner trying to take down his uncle Cole, her brother-in-law, by tackling him around the legs. Cole lifted Tanner over his shoulder firefighter-style and raced around the fenced-in backyard next to the ranch house.

"Everything okay?" Macey, her older sister, joined her at the window. "You were quiet at dinner."

Macey's dark hair had been pulled up in a messy bun out of reach from her young son's chubby fingers, who napped against her chest.

She swayed lightly as she rubbed circles over his tiny back.

"Your husband is great with kids." Mallory glanced at her, then returned her attention to Cole, who set Tanner back on his feet. He chased his six-year-old daughter, Lexi, whose giggles echoed Tanner's.

"Yes, he is. Lexi and Deacon are blessed to have him as a dad." The look of love on her sister's face caused an ache in Mallory's chest.

She had that once. For a brief time.

"They have a pretty great mom, too—but then again, I'm a little biased." Mallory slid an arm around Macey's shoulders and gave her a side hug.

"Thanks, birthday girl. You're pretty great yourself. I'm glad you're back home where you belong."

Unexpected tears filled Mallory's eyes.

She appreciated her sister's words, but *was* she where she belonged?

An image of Jonah swam through her head, and she cleared that thought immediately.

"What's going on here?" Bear, Macey's fraternal twin, rested his bent elbows on each of his sisters' shoulders.

Mallory blinked several times, then eyed her brother. "Just talking about how Cole needs to be nominated for Father of the Year."

Bear jerked back, his face twisted in mock

hurt. "Hey, now. He's not the only dad in the group. What about me?"

"Or me?" Wyatt, Mallory's other older brother, joined them.

Mallory turned, looked her dark-haired brothers up and down, and tapped a finger against her chin. "Okay, fine. You're both in the running too."

If only her own son could say the same thing about his own father.

Why, oh why, did Jonah have to show up now? Just as she was trying to get her life back together?

Mallory pushed past her brothers, who were built like linebackers, and returned to the sink. She picked up one of the plates left on the counter and scraped the remnants of frosting and melted ice cream into the compost bucket. After adding it to the dishwasher, she reached for another and repeated the process.

"Mal, you scrape any harder and you're going to take the paint off the plate." Wyatt placed his hands on her shoulders.

Mallory jumped and dropped the plate. It shattered all over the floor. "What?" Whirling around, she cringed at the bite in her tone.

Hands up in front of him, he took a step back. "Whoa. Sorry. I didn't mean to startle you."

Shaking her head, Mallory dropped the fork in the utensil holder, then stepped over the shards and retrieved the broom from the pantry. "No, it's not you."

"What's going on?" He crouched and started picking up pieces of the broken plate.

The concern in her brother's voice tugged at the loose thread barely holding her emotions together. No matter how quickly she blinked, she couldn't stop the tears from escaping. She pressed her fingers against her eyes.

Wyatt took the broom from her, then gathered her against his chest.

For a moment, she allowed the feelings she'd been holding back since seeing Jonah surface and spill out, soaking her brother's T-shirt.

"Mallory, honey, what's wrong?" Mom placed a hand on her back.

Mallory sucked in a few breaths. She reached for a dish towel and dried her face. She kept her gaze on her freshly polished toes and shook her head. "Sorry."

"Never apologize for your emotions. Something triggered those tears."

She looked at Mom and found her family had gathered in the kitchen, watching her.

Bear wrapped an arm around Piper, his wife, who'd just learned she was pregnant. Callie, Wyatt's wife of six months, moved beside him and linked her arm through his. Dad leaned a shoulder against the fridge. Macey remained by the window, swaying to keep her son asleep, but turned and faced them.

Great. Just what she needed—an audience.

But they were her family. The ones she leaned on the most, especially over the past six months.

She blew out a breath. "Can we go into the living room? I need to tell you something."

She ducked between her two brothers so she didn't have to see the looks of pity on their faces. She took the broom from Wyatt and swept up the mess while her family moved out of the way.

After emptying the dustpan of broken pieces into the trash, she headed into the living room. Rosie jumped off the couch and stood next to her.

Facing the fireplace, with its generations of names etched into the stones, Mallory located her stone, surrounded by names of her siblings, and traced the letters.

"Mallory?"

She turned and found her family sitting on the dark leather couch and matching chairs.

She shoved her hands in her pockets. "I've been keeping something from you for years."

Her parents glanced at each other, then looked at her with matching frowns.

Mallory sucked in her lips and rolled her eyes toward the ceiling to prevent more tears from leaking out again. "I know you guys weren't pleased when I refused to tell you who Tanner's father was. At that time, I had my reasons and asked you to honor them." She pulled in a breath, then let it out slowly. "What I didn't tell you was Tanner's father and I had eloped. Tanner wasn't born out of wedlock, as I led you to believe."

Mom's eyes widened. "Why would you keep something like that from us? We're your family. There's nothing you could say that would change that."

The disappointment on her mother's face nearly choked Mallory. She dropped her chin to her chest, then shook her head. Rosie leaned against her leg.

Swallowing several times, she looked at her family, paused on her brother Bear, then swung her gaze back to her parents. "He deployed shortly after we got married…and sent divorce papers a few weeks later. Then I learned I was pregnant. He didn't respond when I asked him to contact me."

Mom slid off the arm of Dad's recliner and moved to Mallory, wrapping her arms around her. "I'm so very sorry. You could've told us. We would've been there for you."

Mallory nodded, not trusting her voice for a moment. Her eyes welled again. "I know you would have. I was humiliated, embarrassed, angry, scared. I signed the papers and didn't hear from him again. Until today."

"Today?" Mom pulled back. "When?"

"I visited Bri and Cam. And he was there. He's Cam's cousin."

"Wait a minute." Bear leaned forward in his chair and rested his elbows on his knees. "Jonah Hayes is Tanner's dad?"

"You knew he was Cam's cousin?"

"Of course. Jonah was my best friend for years. I'm surprised you didn't know."

Heat spread across Mallory's face. "You're several years older than me. You were off doing rodeo stuff while I was still in school. Cam's from Durango and didn't move here until he married Bri, which happened while I was still in the navy and wasn't able to get leave to attend. How would I know about Cam's family?"

"True enough." Bear curled his fingers into fists, his face thunderous. "I'm gonna kill him."

Mallory pushed out of her mother's embrace and strode over to her brother, crossing her arms over her chest. "Stay out of this. I will handle it."

"He hurt my sister and my nephew."

"I mean it, Bear. This isn't your fight. Besides, there's more."

"Like what?" Dad's deep but calm voice pulled her attention away from her brother.

She heaved a sigh and looked at him. "Jonah didn't file the paperwork."

"So that means…" Dad raised an eyebrow.

"I'm still married." Saying the words out loud

made her stomach tighten. "Apparently, my lawyer didn't think to notify me of that fact."

Pushing to his feet, Bear lifted his hands and dropped them back at his sides. "Congratulations?"

"I wouldn't go that far. Jonah's back in town, claiming to be a changed man, and wants a second chance at making our marriage work. And being a father to Tanner."

"He's seven years too late on that, isn't he?"

"Until today, he didn't know about Tanner."

"Why not? I've been deployed. I still received mail. Not to mention e-mail and video chats." Wyatt stood and moved next to Bear.

Her brothers. Her protectors. The two who'd taught her to stand up for herself. Thankfully, they hadn't been around to see her greatest failure.

Mallory shared what details Jonah had told her. Despite her feelings toward the man, her chest ached when she thought of what he must have endured.

"A couple of years ago, Leland arrived late to our men's Bible study. Said Jonah had contacted him after not hearing from him for several years. During that time, Leland didn't know if he was alive or not. Jonah had been busted up pretty bad. Almost didn't make it. Had countless surgeries on his back just to be able to walk again. Spent some time in rehab, then went dark for quite a while." Dad rubbed a hand over his jaw. "Leland mentioned a farm in Pennsylvania where Jonah had given his life to the Lord and wanted a fresh start."

Bear looked at their dad, then took a step toward Mallory. "I know he hurt you, and I'm sorry for that. Just keep in mind that maybe he didn't ignore your request to talk."

Mallory's shoulders slumped as the weight of her brother's words pressed on her.

That was in the past.

She needed to focus on her future. On her son's future.

She shared Bri's house-sitting request, Cam's desire to sell the farm and Jonah's suggestion to buy it together. She lifted her shoulders and held out her hands. "What do I do?"

Dad pushed to his feet and shoved one weathered hand in his pocket. "Mal, what's the Lord leading you to do?"

She shook her head. "I don't know."

"Have you asked Him?"

Leave it to her dad to cut to the chase.

"Not really." Should she confess she hadn't exactly been listening to the Lord since He'd seemed to turn a deaf ear to her when that intruder broke into her apartment and took her and her son hostage?

"Maybe you should." He waved a hand over their family. "Each one of us has been given a second chance with life. And your brothers and sister have second chances at rebuilding the lives they've always wanted. Don't you think Jonah deserves a second chance too? And what about Tanner? He deserves the opportunity to get to know his father." Dad reached for her hand. "And this time, you won't be alone. We'll be there to offer any support you may need."

She looked at her father's face, so kind and calm. Deep lines and a permanent tan from years spent outside. But the peace in his blue eyes made her yearn for the same thing.

When was the last time she felt peace?

Not since the hostage situation and the nightmares began. Not since she needed a canine companion to help with her anxiety. Not since she'd left her naval career behind and sought solace at the ranch.

Would giving Jonah a second chance give her the serenity she'd been craving? Tanner did deserve to get to know his father. Maybe Dad was right and she needed to give the guy an opportunity to prove himself.

But this time, Mallory refused to allow Jonah to break her heart again.

Mallory was the last person Jonah expected to be standing on his father's front porch when he answered the door.

After ushering her and her beautiful dog inside, and despite his repeated invitations to sit, she stood in the middle of his father's living room.

The ache in his lower back and right hip had him wanting to return to the recliner, where he'd been sitting before the doorbell rang. But he'd stand for as long as she did.

Now he needed to keep his foot out of his mouth and let her talk.

Instead, he shoved his hand in his right pocket and ran his other over his face. "Just so I understand what you're saying—you want to buy the farm. By yourself. Not partner with me."

"That's right. That way, I won't lose everything again when you decide I'm not worth staying around for."

Her words slammed into his chest.

He eyed her. "You don't trust easily, do you?"

"I trusted you enough to marry you. Once. Now I'm cautious. Like I said—it's not just about me anymore."

"Right—your other condition. I can see my son as long as you're present." His jaw tightened.

"Jonah, he doesn't even know you." Her eyes softened. "I won't keep you from him. You're welcome to see him any time you want, but it must be at the ranch or someplace in town with me or one of my family members present. He needs to get to know you."

As much as he wanted to argue about that restriction, Mallory had every right to be wary. He'd been the one who abandoned her.

She didn't know about the years of being in and out of hospitals, enduring excruciating pain and mental anguish because he shut her out of his life because he'd been a coward.

"No, I get it. I haven't been around many kids, and I don't have the slightest clue in how to parent."

"You'll learn. Tanner's a good kid. A sweet boy who loves animals, being outside and riding. He wants to be a bull rider when he grows up."

Jonah raised an eyebrow. "Is that so?"

Mallory held up a hand. "I have time to change his mind, hopefully. He's only seven."

"Does Vic still do the Lil Riders group? Maybe we could get him enrolled in that."

"Bear took it over, and Tanner's been a part of it since he was five. He lived with my parents while I was on sea duty. The group helped him with missing me."

"Your parents have always been supportive."

"Yes, they have. In fact, Dad and Bear are the ones who suggested I give you another chance. For Tanner's sake, of course."

"They're good men."

"The best. I use them as measuring sticks for the guys in my life."

If she compared him to her father and brothers, then Jonah wouldn't make it past the one-millimeter mark. But more than that, it was the plural of the noun she used.

"Guys? Is there someone else? Is that why you won't give me a second chance to prove I've changed?"

Shaking her head, she kept her eyes fixed on the leash she ran through her hands. "There's no one else. I haven't seen you in nearly eight years. You show up with no warning, and all of a sudden, you want a second chance. I signed the papers once, ending our marriage. As far as I'm concerned, we are no longer husband and wife."

"The state of Virginia may argue that point."

Sighing, Mallory folded her arms over her chest. "I won't argue with you every time we're in the same room. I didn't grow up that way, and I refuse to allow Tanner to as well. We'll need to find a way to get along. I want him to get to know you, but I can't have you fixating on us." She waved her finger between the two of them.

He held up his hands. "Fine. Okay. I accept your decision about Tanner. I want to get to know him. I see your point about doing it where he feels comfortable. I get that you're not ready to pick up where we left off. I don't like it, but I accept that too. But I refuse to allow you to buy the farm on your own. Sure, you could get Cam and Bri to sell it to you."

Mallory held out her hands as if they were scales trying to be balanced. "Cam is your cousin and Bri is my best friend." She dropped them at her sides. "I know how that's going to play out if they have to choose who to sell the farm to."

Jonah took a tentative step toward her, but Rosie moved in front of her. With a sigh, he stopped. "It's not a competition, Mal. Let's partner together. We can have paperwork drawn up to protect ourselves so neither one of us loses should we decide it's not working and need to sell. We're investing in our son's future. And the lives of others. What do you say?"

Still holding Rosie's leash, Mallory and Rosie wandered around the living room, pausing in front of the bookcase where his father's favorite Louis L'Amour and Zane Grey novels lined the shelves. Then she turned back to him, her expression neutral, but something flashed in her eyes.

Hope?

In his dreams, maybe.

"I don't know. I need to think about it. And talk to the bank. It's a big decision."

"I get that." He tried to keep his voice from sounding like an eager ten-year-old promised his favorite video game.

"I'll give you a decision soon. In the meantime, we'll co-parent Tanner. Until you get to know him better, I will have final say when it comes to his medical care and all of that."

"When can I meet him?"

Mallory's head jerked up. "Meet him?"

Jonah lifted a shoulder. "I have to meet him in order to get to know him. Better before we move into the farmhouse together."

Mallory flipped up her hands. "First, you can meet him whenever you want. Second, we are *not* moving into the farmhouse together. If you want to live there, that's fine. I'll find somewhere else for Tanner and me. There's a small cabin on the property. We'll live there."

Even though he hadn't seen the cabin and had been inside the farmhouse only once, Cam had described the cabin as rustic. Somehow, he couldn't see Mallory living in "rustic."

He rubbed the back of his neck. "I'll take the cabin. You two will be much more comfortable at the house. I'd like to meet Tanner tonight, if that's okay?"

"Sure, why don't you come by after dinner? We're having brownie sundaes for dessert."

After dinner. Not an invitation to share the family table. But he got it.

He nodded, then he touched her arm. "And you and me?"

She glanced at his fingers, then back at his face, her brows pulled together. "What about us?"

"How will you explain us to Tanner?"

"Tanner will know you are his father, and we are married. As far as our future is concerned, we will be...friends."

"Friends."

"It's a start."

Not what he'd wanted, but Mallory was right. She could've turned her back on him, but instead, she was giving him the chance he'd requested.

As for their marriage, he had a bigger fight ahead. But he was up for the challenge. If she never forgave him, he'd have to find a way to live with that. Somehow.

Chapter Three

When was the last time he had been this nervous?

Jonah drove through the gate leading to the Stone River Ranch. The dirt road separated the pastures where grazing cattle lifted their heads as he passed.

The stone-and-timber ranch house came into view as he slowed and drove around the semicircle and parked next to the Stone River Ranch truck.

When he closed his door, he wasn't surprised to find Deacon, Bear and Wyatt Stone sitting on the front porch.

Even though the men rocked casually in the hickory chairs, he'd have to get past them before he could meet his son.

He ran a hand over his hair, still damp from his shower. Good thing he'd gotten it cut yesterday. He'd taken the time to press his light blue button-down but left it untucked.

The ache in his lower back clawed at him, but

he tried to ignore it. As his boot touched the bottom step, he locked eyes with Mallory's oldest brother. "Bear, good to see you again."

"Jonah. It's been a while."

Bear and Wyatt stood at the same time, feet apart and arms crossed over their chests.

He got the whole big-brother-intimidation act. If he had a little sister, he would've been the same way. As it was, he wanted to do what he could to help Cam.

Somehow, he had to show he'd changed and wasn't there to hurt anyone, especially Mallory and Tanner.

Tanner.

Still blew his mind that he had a kid.

One he was going to meet any minute now.

Deacon Stone, Mallory's father, met Jonah at the top of the steps and held out a hand. "Jonah, welcome to Stone River."

Jonah shook the older man's weathered hand. "Thank you, sir. I have no intention of hurting Mallory or Tanner. I'm not the man you used to know. All I'm asking for is a chance."

The older man smiled, lines deepening at the corners of his blue eyes. "Around here, we believe in second chances." He glanced at his sons. "Right, boys?"

Bear's face remained stony, but he relaxed his posture. He gave a curt nod.

Wyatt stepped forward and held out a hand. "Jonah."

His firm grip and the way his jaw tightened were Wyatt's ways of warning him not to mess with his family.

Jonah just wanted to make things right.

He needed to address why he left. Why his fear of failing her and messing up her life caused him to panic. He'd been so hurt when his own mother walked out on their family, yet he'd done the same thing. Instead of trusting Mal and opening up and risking being vulnerable, he'd simply left. He filed for divorce like a coward.

But God had given him a second chance. In life and with Mallory and his son. Now he could fix what he'd broken.

Once he got past the gatekeepers, there was hope of doing that.

The front door opened, and Mallory stood in the doorway.

Jonah's mouth dried as his pulse picked up speed.

She wore a flowered skirt that touched the top of her knees and a matching light blue T-shirt. Her hair was gathered in a messy knot on top of her head. The ever-faithful Rosie appeared at her side.

He brushed past her dad and brothers and started to reach for her. Then he dropped his hands. What was he supposed to do? Shake her hand? Give her a hug? A kiss was certainly out of the question.

Jonah shoved his hand into his pocket and cleared his throat. "Mallory, it's good to see you again. Thank you for inviting me."

Tucking her hands beneath her arms, her mouth tightened as she stared at him a moment, then she turned to her family. "Can I have a minute alone with Jonah?"

Mr. Stone jerked his head toward the open front door, where conversation and laughter spilled onto the porch. "Come on, boys. Let's give your sister some privacy."

The last one into the house, Bear shot Jonah a warning look, then closed the door behind him.

Mallory stepped onto the porch, and Rosie followed. "I told Tanner about you, and he's pretty excited. He may have a lot of questions. Just go easy. He's kind of shy at first."

"Of course. What do you think I'm going to do?"

She shrugged and stared over his shoulder.

He held out a hand. "Listen, I get it. This is new for all of us. I'm the one who screwed up, but you don't have to worry. I won't do anything to hurt Tanner. You have my word."

She looked at him. "Giving your word and keeping it are two different things."

"So you've said. Repeatedly. How about giving me a chance?"

She lifted a brow as the corner of her mouth tilted up. "You're here, aren't you?"

"I appreciate that."

Mallory reached for the doorknob. "Come inside and have some ice cream."

Jonah followed her into the house, his throat tightening with each step. The scent of warm chocolate swirled in the air.

As they entered the kitchen, laughter and talking funneled around them.

Mrs. Stone looked up and smiled. She handed the ice-cream scoop to her husband and walked toward him, her arms outstretched. "Jonah Hayes, look at you all grown up."

As she wrapped her arms around him, Jonah breathed in scents of vanilla and sunshine. Her genuine welcome loosened the band around his chest. "Hey, Mrs. Stone. You haven't changed a bit."

She gave him a playful swat on the chest and shot him a smile that reminded him so much of Mallory during their time together. "Flatterer. But I'll take it."

"Want some ice cream? Deac's scooping."

"Brownies and ice cream. Two of my favorite things."

"Then you're very fortunate."

Oh, she had no idea.

A young boy with dark hair falling over his

forehead ran over to the table, a bowl in his hand. "Papa, can I have sprinkles on my ice cream?"

Mr. Stone slid a large jar of colorful sprinkles across the table to him. "Sure thing, Tanner."

Tanner.

His son.

His heart slammed against his ribs so hard Jonah was sure everyone must've heard it. His eyes scoured the boy's face, taking in the freckles on his nose, his warm brown eyes and the slight dimple in his cheek when the kid smiled.

He looked so much like Jonah had as a child.

No way could he deny paternity. Not that he planned to.

Mallory touched Tanner's shoulder, leaned over and whispered something in his ear. The boy's head shot up, his wide eyes connecting with Jonah's.

Slowly, he set his bowl on the table, next to the container of sprinkles, then walked over to Jonah. "So, you're my dad."

Even though he hadn't asked a question, Tanner's voice held a sense of…wonder, maybe?

Jonah crouched in front of him, ignoring the screaming in his lower back. "Yes, I am." Not knowing what else to do, he stuck out his hand. "I'm Jonah Hayes."

Tanner looked at it for a moment, then placed his small hand in Jonah's. "Hi, I'm Tanner Stone."

Stone.

Of course.

More than anything, Jonah wanted to yank the young boy into his arms, hold him close and beg for forgiveness for not being there when he needed him. Instead, he nodded.

"What do I call you?"

Jonah shrugged. He hadn't thought of that. "What would you like to call me?"

Tanner cocked his head, scrunched up his right eye and twisted his mouth as he tapped his chin. "I've always wanted a dad. Now you're here." He threw out his hands. "That's like a birthday wish come true. Can I call you *Dad*?"

An unexpected lump formed in Jonah's throat as his vision blurred. Swallowing several times, he nodded. "Of course. I'd love that."

He did not deserve this kid.

Tanner grabbed Jonah's hand. "Come on, Dad. Let's get some ice cream. Papa lets me have as many sprinkles as I want."

And like that, Tanner seemed to accept him.

He allowed his son to tug him toward the table. "This is my dad." Tanner pointed at three little girls sitting at a small children's table with colorful cups of ice cream in front of them. "That's Avery. She's eight and a half and a little bossy. That's Lexi. She's six and likes cats. And that's Mia. She's three and dances a lot."

Jonah laughed as he crouched at the table with the three girls. "Ladies, it's nice to meet you."

Avery looked at him. "So if you're Tanner's dad, how come I haven't met you before? Does that mean you're married to my aunt Mallory?"

Heat climbed up Jonah's throat. He exchanged glances with Mallory, who simply watched with an amused expression on her face.

"You haven't met me before because I haven't been here before."

"Why not?"

"Because sometimes adults make choices that are hard to understand."

"Oh, okay." The little girl turned back to her ice cream. She scooped up a drippy swirl of vanilla and chocolate and held it out to him. "Want a bite of ice cream?"

"That looks really good, but I don't want to take your ice cream." He smiled at her. "How about if I get my own?"

She nodded, then shoved the spoon in her mouth and smiled at him.

Jonah pushed to his feet, moved next to Mallory and blew out a breath.

She leaned close, her lips barely touching his ear. "And you thought my brothers would be tough."

He laughed. "Nothing like the honesty of a child, right?"

"You got it." Mallory handed him a bowl and a spoon, then waved him in front of her. "Help yourself."

He reached for a brownie and found they were still warm. He accepted two scoops of vanilla ice cream from Mr. Stone, swirled a spoon of hot fudge over top and added a sprinkle of chopped nuts. He grabbed a napkin and turned.

Mallory's family had taken most of the spots in the open living room.

Where was he supposed to sit?

As if reading his mind, Mallory's mom laid a hand on his shoulder, then pointed to an empty cushion on the couch. "Jonah, there's an open seat next to Mallory."

Shooting Mallory what he hoped was an apologetic glance, Jonah sat, his lower back begging him to sink into the deep cushion, but he straightened and pressed as much of his body toward the arm of the couch as he could. That way, he didn't need to be touching Mallory. No matter how much he wanted to.

He dug into his sundae, savoring the melted ice cream over the warm brownie. Around him, Mallory's family talked and laughed as metal spoons scraped against the glass bowls.

"So, Jonah, I hear you spent some time in Pennsylvania." Mr. Stone sat his empty bowl on the side table and leaned forward, resting his elbows on his knees.

"Yes, at a dairy farm run by a man and his four sons. They created a program to help disabled vets learn farming skills so they can find a purpose again as civilians."

Mr. Stone reached for a tablet. He flipped open the cover and scrolled on the screen. "Yes. Here it is." He held up the electronic device so Jonah could see. "I read an article about them recently in one of my farm-and-ranch magazines. They're doing great work. They said they started the project to bring their brother home."

Jonah nodded. "Their youngest, Micah—he lost an arm while serving overseas. IED. He and I have similar stories, even though I came home with all my limbs intact. He was messed up for a while—again, like me. Then he returned home and ended up starting a program called A Hand Up, which is a transitional home for veterans looking for a second chance. I spent time there, and the Hollands have inspired me to start something similar out this way."

Bear pushed to his feet, collected his dad's empty bowl and reached for Jonah's. "So that's why you came back home?"

"I came home because it was time." Jonah stood, locking eyes with Bear. "My cousin is going through a stressful time, and I wanted to help him out."

"By buying his farm?"

"Maybe. That was my original intent. But there have been some unexpected…" His voice trailed off. What could he say? He wouldn't really call them *complications*. Or *challenges*. "Unexpected opportunities. So I just have to wait and see where the Lord is leading me."

Mr. Stone joined them and clapped a hand on Jonah's shoulder. "Well, you'll never go wrong by listening to Him."

Tanner moved away from the small table where he was sitting with his cousins and stood in front of Mallory. He pressed his hands on her knees and leaned forward. "Mom, I'm done. Can I take Dad outside and show him the horses?"

Mallory pulled Tanner onto her lap, then glanced up at Jonah. "Want to see the horses?"

"Yes, of course." Jonah sat on the edge of the couch. "Would you like to have horses when we move to the farm?"

Tanner's head jerked up as his face twisted into a frown. "What farm?" Then his eyes widened as he swiveled back to Mallory and jumped to his feet. "Are we moving? I don't want to move. I want to stay at the ranch. My room is here. Papa needs my help in the barn. Said he couldn't do it without me."

Mallory closed her eyes a moment and pulled in a deep breath. Then she exhaled and looked at Jonah, her eyes sharp and mouth tight. "I haven't talked to Tanner about the farm yet. I figured letting him know his dad was in town was enough for him to deal with for one day."

Jonah dropped his forehead into his palm.

Nothing like opening his big mouth and upsetting his son the first time he met him. What kind of father was he going to be? Was he even cut out for this?

Well, he needed to learn quickly because he wasn't walking away. He was here to stay. And Mallory would have to get used to him being back in her life, no matter how she felt about him.

For now, though, he'd settle for fixing things with his son. No way did he want to mess that up.

Well, that didn't go as Mallory had hoped.

With the VA loan paperwork from the bank tucked into her purse, she walked to the end of the block to her aunt's diner.

Bells clanged against the glass as she opened the door and stepped inside. She breathed in the scent of sizzling fries, fresh coffee, and sugar emanating from the bakery case by the register. Forks scraping against plates and the buzz of conversation filtered through the air.

Aunt Lynetta rounded the counter and held out her arms. "Hey, sweet girl, how you doing?"

A navy *Netta's Diner* apron covered her aunt's curvy figure. Her dark hair, the same color as Mallory's, had been pulled up into a messy bun and secured with her signature yellow pencil.

Mallory pasted a smile on her face. "Fine. I'm meeting Bri for lunch."

Aunt Lynetta eyed her. "Your mouth says you're

fine, but your eyes tell a different story." She pulled her toward the coffee counter and patted one of the red vinyl stools. "Sit and tell me what's going on."

Laughing softly and shaking her head, Mallory did as instructed. She rested an elbow on the counter and looked at her aunt. "I could never put anything past you. I just left the bank. I've been preapproved for a small VA loan, but I don't know if it's enough to buy the farm. My credit is great, but my monthly income is low. Plus, there are inspections and all that before the loan is guaranteed."

"The farm? What farm?"

Mallory bit the corner of her lip, then lowered her head closer to her aunt's ear. "Bri asked me to farm-sit for the summer, but she's seriously thinking of selling the fruit farm. If she does decide, I want to be able to hand her a check and take ownership. But keep that between us, please. My family knows and that's it."

Aunt Lynetta released a tiny squeal, then covered her mouth with her hands. "Oh, honey. That's just great. Surely your parents will help you with the rest if you need it. Look what they've done for your brothers and sister." She jerked a head toward the kitchen. "If they can't, then Uncle Pete and I will help you."

Mallory grabbed her aunt's arms. "You are so

sweet, but no. I have to do this on my own. Besides, there are some complications…"

Aunt Lynetta's eyebrow shot up. "What kind of complications?"

Mallory toyed with a clean spoon on the counter and filled her aunt in on the details of the past few days.

The older woman wasn't quiet too often, but now she looked like someone had punched her in the stomach as she continued to open her mouth, then close it again. She blinked. Then her eyes narrowed as she pressed a hand against her chest. "Well, now. That wasn't news I was expecting."

Aunt Lynetta moved behind the counter, filled a clean cup with coffee and slid it to Mallory. "So, what are you gonna do?"

Mallory emptied two sugar packets and a splash of cream into the cup and stirred. She tapped the spoon on the rim and then set it on a clean napkin. "I don't know yet. Jonah and I have a lot to discuss. We're completely different people than we were eight years ago."

"You get to know each other all over again." Aunt Lynetta leaned on the counter.

"You make it sound so simple."

"No, it's not simple. I get that. But you have a son together, and you don't want to complicate that."

"But I don't trust him. I have to protect Tanner too."

"If he's changed, then give him a chance to prove himself."

The diner door opened again, and Bri stepped inside.

"Bri's here. Thanks for listening. And for your wisdom." Mallory gave her aunt a hug, then slid off the stool and grabbed her purse and her coffee.

"Think about what I said, honey. We all need second chances."

"Thanks. I will."

She and Bri settled into a booth near the window that overlooked Main Street.

Once the server had taken Bri's drink order, she folded her hands on the paper place mat that also served as a menu. "So, what did the bank say?"

Mallory pulled the folded papers from her purse. "I don't qualify for as much as I had hoped. Because of my current income, they would only prequalify me a portion of what you're asking. If I want to get a VA loan, then there are inspections that need to be done. Jonah and I talked about putting in half, but I still hoped to be able to buy the whole thing."

"That's disappointing for you, I'm sure." Bri paused while the server set her iced tea with lemon on the table and placed a glass of water in front of Mallory. Bri smiled her thanks, then pulled the wrapper off her straw. She let out a sigh. "We have another problem as well."

Mallory's stomach tightened. "What's that?"

"Cam wants to sell the farm to his cousin."

She expected that to happen, so why did Bri's revelation still surprise her?

"Even though Jonah wants me to partner with him?" Mallory stabbed her straw against the table.

"Yes."

Mallory's shoulders sagged as her dream of owning the farm dissipated.

"Even though you're like the sister I never had, he wants to keep it in our family. Not only that, but he called in an appraiser after we talked about selling it. Apparently, the farm is worth more than what I had originally thought...and told you." She lifted her glass and eyed Mallory over the rim. "A lot more. Which surprised both Cam and me. We also were contacted by a commercial buyer who is willing to pay cash."

"How did the buyer learn about the farm? You really want the farm to go to someone commercial?"

Bri waved away Mallory's questions. "No, not at all. I don't even know how he found out about it." She folded her hands in her lap and sagged against the booth. "But how do we decide between you and Jonah?"

"Jonah must've changed his mind about both of us putting in half." Mallory squeezed her lemon, stirred it into her water and lifted a shoulder. "I may be able to talk to my parents and go through them for a loan for the rest, but I really wanted to do this on my own."

Bri's eyes glistened as she grabbed Mallory's hand. "I know. I'm sorry. I just want to stop fighting with Cam over everything and have peace so we can get our marriage back to where it used to be."

The server returned to take their order, but Mallory's appetite had vanished. She ordered a club sandwich, knowing she'd end up taking most of it home.

The bells above the door clanked against the glass. Bri's eyes lit up. Mallory turned and found Cam and Jonah walking toward them.

"What are they doing here?" she hissed to Bri.

Bri shrugged, then slid across the red vinyl seat, making room for her husband. Jonah stood at the end of their table and looked at Mallory.

Releasing another sigh, quieter this time, she slid closer to the window, taking her place mat, coffee and water with her.

He settled in next to her and slipped his arm over the back of the booth. And shot her a smile. "Thanks."

"Don't mention it."

Cam folded his hands on the table and glanced between Mallory and Bri. "Sorry to interrupt your lunch, but this couldn't wait. Jonah and I were talking. We had an idea and wanted to run it past the two of you."

"What's that?" Bri slid her hand in between her husband's.

"Well, I was telling Jonah about the buyer and how we don't really want to go commercial. He reminded me of his offer to buy, but then I mentioned the appraiser's figure, which is more than what he can afford right now. He also mentioned Mal wants the farm, too, but she wasn't thrilled about partnering with him. So we came up with the plan that you two—" Cam broke off and wagged a finger between Jonah and Mallory "—can run the farm for the summer. The strawberry beds have been replanted. The apple trees were trimmed recently. If you can turn it around and show potential, then whoever can afford it at the end of—oh, let's say June—will be given the first option to buy."

Mallory turned to Jonah and lowered her voice. "Is he seriously talking about a competition?"

Jonah lowered his mouth close to her ear. "No. Just listen. This isn't about us. It's to help them."

Mallory ground her teeth together and reached for her glass, sloshing liquid over the side. Jonah handed her a napkin.

"During the next two months, you'll be able to see if the farm is too much work and if you can still stand the sight of each other." Cam grinned.

Mallory had no sense of humor when it came to Jonah. She didn't want to be around him now. But this wasn't about her. She had a son, who'd spent the past couple of days talking about little else but his dad. And her friend longed for peace. Something Mallory understood too well.

"If you change your mind about the farm, then I'll contact the commercial buyer and sell it to him." Cam ran his thumb over Bri's knuckles and turned to her. "Either way, you and I will be out from under it. We can start looking for a house in Durango. Maybe even do a little traveling before I take the job Dad's offering. We haven't had time for a vacation since our honeymoon."

Bri's eyes widened. "Are you serious?"

Cam pulled her into a side hug. "Of course. I wouldn't joke about something like this."

Her eyes suddenly bright, she looked at Mallory. "What do you think?"

The last thing Mallory wanted was to crush her friend's hope. And she didn't want the Wallen Family Fruit Farm to be sold to a commercial buyer either.

But agreeing to Cam's idea meant partnering with Jonah for the next two months.

Could she get the rest of the money by the end

of the sixty days? Maybe if she talked to her parents? Or took her aunt up on her offer? It wasn't the most ideal situation, but maybe Jonah wasn't the only one who needed a second chance.

She glanced at her friends, who pressed their foreheads together, and remembered Bri's tears from the other day. Saying yes would help her friend restore what was broken. And it would also give Mallory a place of her own to raise Tanner. Would that be enough to ease the nightmares? Or would this change just bring in new ones?

Mallory didn't want to go down that road right now.

Forcing enthusiasm into her voice, she smiled at Bri. "Okay."

Jonah's head jerked up. "Okay?"

Her jaw tightened again. Nodding, she gave him a long look. "I'm on board with the sixty-day…trial. But my previous conditions still stand."

Jonah thrust his hand at Cam. "Well, cuz, looks like you need to start packing."

Then he wrapped an arm around her shoulder and lowered his mouth to her ear again. "You won't regret this."

Too late.

Regret happened the second she agreed. A band tightened around her chest, making it tough to breathe. She reached down to her knee, but

Rosie wasn't there. She folded her hands in her lap and squeezed her fingers tightly.

Was she making the right choice? For her? Or Tanner? Or even for Jonah?

Only time would tell.

Somehow, she needed to get the rest of the money to secure the loan.

Chapter Four

Moving out of the ranch house and into Bri and Cam's place proved to be harder than Mallory had expected.

For one thing, how had she accumulated so much stuff? Had the boxes multiplied while being stored at the ranch?

At least now she'd have more of her own space, even if it turned out to be temporary. It gave her time to find something more permanent if staying on the farm didn't work out.

Best to have a Plan B.

After hashing out Bri and Cam's expectations for the farm and what they hoped Jonah and Mallory would achieve, they agreed to the plan.

Right now, she needed to plan for bedtime.

Mallory wove through the boxes lining the walls of the Wallen farmhouse, searching for the ones that should've been carried upstairs to the room Tanner had picked out earlier in the week. But when she went to make up his bed, there were no boxes.

She just wanted to give him some sense of normalcy after the busyness of the past two weeks.

Once she and Jonah had talked with him about moving to the fruit farm, he seemed okay, especially when she promised he'd still be able to spend a lot of time at the ranch.

But last night's bedtime conversation still rattled her.

What if they forget me?

Honey, they're your family. They love you. They will never forget you.

Dad did.

She had no answer except to remind him that people made poor choices and now his dad wanted to make up for his mistakes.

Why was convincing her little boy so much easier than her own heart?

She found a box with Tanner's name on the side in his handwriting. She opened it and discovered his favorite comforter and matching sheets, all decorated with a pattern of horseshoes and cowboy hats. The scent of fabric softener drifted from the box.

Mom must've washed it before packing up his room. Bless her.

After a very long day, she'd be able to tuck him into a cozy bed.

Clutching the bedding, she climbed the stairs with Rosie right behind her and headed to the room at the end of the hall. She moved to the bed and dropped the sheets and comforter on the bare mattress.

"Mom?"

She jumped at her son's quiet voice. She turned and found him sitting in the corner of the room with his back to the wall and one of his favorite horses in his hands.

She crossed the room and sat next to him. Rosie made herself comfortable at their feet. "Hey, buddy. Why are you sitting up here by yourself?"

He lifted a shoulder and kept his eyes on Trigger, the black-dotted Appaloosa. "I miss the ranch."

"Babe, we've been gone an hour."

"Yeah, but it's almost dinnertime. What if Papa and Nana can't eat because they miss me too much?"

Mallory wrapped an arm around her son's narrow shoulders and pulled him close. She pressed a kiss to the top of his head. "Would you like to have dinner at the ranch so they will feel better?"

His head jerked up, eyes wide. "You mean it?"

She pushed to her feet. "Sure, let's call Nana."

Tanner jumped up and wrapped his arms around her waist, his cheek pressing against her stomach. "You're the best mom ever."

"That's easy when I have the best kid ever." She reached for his arms and stepped back. "Help me make your bed first so you can have a place to sleep."

The light in Tanner's eyes dimmed. "Right. I'm not gonna be at the ranch tonight."

Mallory knelt in front of him and brushed the hair off his forehead. "Honey, change is hard. I understand that. You're in a different house, a different room, and it's okay for it all to feel weird. Just know you will get used to it. Remember when you lived in Virginia with me? That was different, too, but you adjusted. Then you were sad when we had to leave."

"I didn't want to leave my friends."

"I know. And I think, with a little time, you will get used to being here too. Plus, we can have the family over for dinner, then you can show Avery, Lexi and Mia your new room."

He nodded. "Okay, let's hurry so we can call Nana."

Working together, they stretched the sheets across the bed and covered them with the comforter. Mallory folded the top down.

They headed out to the hall. As they reached the top of the stairs, someone knocked on the door.

"I'll get it." Tanner raced down the steps with Rosie. He flew across the living room and threw the front door open. "Dad! What are you doing here?"

Mallory hurried to the front door and found

Jonah standing on the front porch, holding two paper bags with grease spots smudging the bottom.

Rosie wedged herself between Tanner and Jonah, her nose lifted toward the bags.

"Jonah, hey."

"Hi, Mal. I figured you two would be hungry, so I swung by the diner and grabbed Tanner's favorite chicken fingers and fries. I tried to call, but I didn't get an answer."

Mallory patted her back pocket and found it empty. No wonder she'd missed his call.

She opened the door wider. "Come in."

Jonah stepped into the room, eyed the wall of boxes and smirked. "I like what you've done with the place. It has that post-move feel."

Mallory rolled her eyes and bit back a smile. "My brothers were great at loading and unloading, but they're not so hot on the logistics. I'll get everything moved into the right rooms."

"I'll help too. But first, let's eat." Jonah lifted the bags.

Mallory eyed Tanner. "We—"

Tanner grabbed her hand. "Come on, Mom. Let's show Dad where the kitchen is."

So much for worrying about Papa and Nana not being able to eat because they missed him too much.

Mallory allowed Tanner to pull her into the kitchen.

Jonah set the bags on the counter next to the stove, then glanced at the empty space under the window where Bri's retro table used to sit. "Looks like we need to get a table for in here."

She wasn't going to allow his use of *we* to get under her skin. She'd outfit the farmhouse how she saw fit, thank you very much. Instead of commenting, she glanced out the window and noticed the weathered picnic table on the back patio Bri and Cam had left behind, not needing it in the city. She jerked her thumb toward the door that led out to the backyard. "Even though it's getting dark and probably a little chilly, let's sit outside."

"Sounds good." Jonah pulled a carton out of one of the paper bags and handed it to her. "Figured we could have this for dessert."

Mallory turned the container around and read the label. "Moose Tracks ice cream. My favorite."

"I know." He winked at her.

Was he remembering one of their last nights together? The walk on the beach while they ate ice-cream cones and dared to dream about their future?

Her stomach clenched as her fingers tightened around the carton. She took a step toward him and lowered her voice. "Listen, Jonah, you can't buy your way into our lives."

As soon as the words left her mouth, she regretted them. Especially when the light dimmed in Jonah's eyes.

His jaw tightened. "That thought never crossed my mind. I wanted to offer some comfort for what may be a difficult day. Leaving the ranch will be an adjustment for Tanner. And you. I wanted to do something nice. That's it."

Okay, now *she* was the jerk.

She pressed a hand against his arm and lifted the ice-cream container. "I'm sorry. And thank you. What you did was very thoughtful."

Jonah took a step toward her and brushed her ear with his lips. "Yes, I screwed up, but I'm not a bad guy. Tanner needs to know I'm going to be there for him from now on—for the big things and the small ones. Same for you. If you'll let me."

He stepped back, and Mallory forced herself to not give in to the shiver tickling her spine. After filling her lungs with air, she released her breath, blowing it out slowly. Then she moved to the opposite counter by the sink and rummaged through a basket of kitchen supplies Mom had put together. She grabbed a handful of napkins along with some paper plates, and held them out to Tanner. "Take these to the picnic table, please."

"Sure, Mom. Come on, Dad. I'll show you the way." He waved an arm toward Jonah.

As they headed outside with Rosie staying next

to Tanner, Mallory took a moment to soak in the sudden stillness in the kitchen.

Jonah's presence messed with her the same way it had over eight years ago, when she'd run into him at the NCO club on base. But this time, she wasn't a fresh-faced sailor excited to see a familiar face halfway across the country.

Now she hated that her cynicism jaded her heart, but she couldn't forget the pain of opening that envelope and pulling out those divorce papers.

Never had she felt so unwanted.

And she wouldn't allow herself to relive that pain. Even if it meant keeping the wall intact around her heart. No matter how many kind gestures Jonah offered.

Nothing could kill the feeling in Jonah's heart. Not even Mallory's silence as Tanner chatted about their day while dragging his french fries through a puddle of ketchup.

Having dinner with his kid still didn't seem real, even though he'd spent every day with Tanner since meeting him two weeks ago.

Had it been two weeks already?

With getting paperwork signed and Cam and Bri moved to Durango, the time had passed in a blur. Too fast. Jonah wanted to hold on to every minute.

But like he told Mallory—repeatedly—he wasn't going anywhere. He was there to stay.

The evening sky blended in shades of blue, purple and orange as the sun slipped behind the San Juan Mountains. Crickets chirped as he climbed the hill to the cabin.

His lower back screamed, but the pain was worth it. For tonight, at least. Maybe he'd have to start driving down to the house.

Whistling, he pushed open the door to the cabin and flicked on the overhead light. Something swooped and flapped over his head.

Perhaps the term "rustic" that Cam had used was a little too generous. With the exception of electricity and running water, the cabin was downright primitive and outdated.

He'd slept in worse, so he was grateful for a place to lay his head.

A braided oval rug covered the wooden floor in front of the kitchenette. A worn plaid couch with sunken cushions sat in front of the window overlooking one of the pastures.

A musty, ammonia-like smell filtered through the stale air. Jonah wrinkled his nose as he moved into the room. Small seedlike droppings littered the floor.

Jonah blew out a breath.

He'd been so busy trying to get Mallory and Tanner moved that he hadn't thought about airing out the cabin.

He crossed the room and turned on the lamp next to the double bed. A flapping sound jerked his eyes to the ceiling as a bat flew out of the corner and came for him.

He ducked, and the bat escaped through the open door.

Ugh. Now what?

The creatures didn't bother him, but he didn't want to sleep with one in the room. As he eyed the bed, he realized the stained mattress would need to be replaced before he could make it.

He glanced at his watch, then moved back to the door. A light shone in the living room window of the farmhouse.

Jonah stepped onto the covered porch, closed the door behind him and headed back down the hill. He reached the farmhouse porch and lifted his hand to knock, then paused.

What was he doing?

There was no way Mallory would believe he wasn't trying to horn in on her living space.

He turned away and started for the front steps. He'd deal with the bats for one night, then figure out a better solution tomorrow after some sleep.

The step creaked as he added his weight.

The door opened.

"Jonah?"

He turned, feeling a little ridiculous.

Mallory stood in the doorway, her arms folded over her chest. "What are you doing?"

Jonah dragged a hand over his weary face, then let out a short laugh that sounded more like a choke. "There are bats in the cabin."

"Bats." She rested a shoulder against the door frame and lifted an eyebrow.

"Yes, bats. The place reeks and needs to be cleaned before I can move in. And I need to buy a new mattress. Could I crash on your couch?" He threw up a hand. "Just for tonight. I promise. Then tomorrow, I can tackle the bat problem."

She eyed him a moment, then stepped back and waved him inside. As he passed, he caught a whiff of something citrusy.

She closed the door behind her, then pressed her back against it. "Umm, the couch is mine. At least for tonight. I didn't have the energy to dig out more bedding. You can sleep in the small apartment off the dining room. The bed's not made up, but Bri left sheets and blankets in the closet."

"Apartment?"

She waved for him to follow her as she turned on lights and moved through the empty dining room filled with more boxes. She opened a set of French doors, turned on a light and stepped into the room.

He followed and found a sitting area with a recliner, love seat and TV. A tiny kitchen contained a small fridge, cooktop and single-bowl sink.

Mallory opened a wooden door. "This is the

bedroom. There's also a small bathroom. After Bri's grandpa died, her dad built this addition so that her grandma would have her own space. They were close enough in case she needed help."

Jonah eyed the double bed and longed to drop onto the covered mattress. "You sleep here, and I'll take the couch."

She shook her head. "I want to be able to hear Tanner if he wakes up. You can sleep here for tonight."

Her emphasis on the last word wasn't lost on him. He'd take what he could get. "Thanks, Mal. I appreciate it. I'll grab my sleeping bag and be out of your hair before you and Tanner get up in the morning."

"No rush. Tanner's a rancher's grandkid—he's up before Mom's roosters. Which is why I go to bed soon after him."

Jonah heard a thump overhead. He pointed to the ceiling. "He's not in bed yet, I take it?"

"He was brushing his teeth and getting his pajamas on. Then I was going to read him a story."

Jonah shifted on his feet. "Mind if I say goodnight?"

Mallory hesitated, then shook her head again. She waved toward the door. "I'm sure he'll be thrilled."

Not giving Mallory a chance to change her mind, Jonah hurried toward the staircase that separated the living room from the dining room and took the steps two at a time.

At the top, he headed down the hall toward the light and found Tanner dressed in blue-and-red-plaid pajamas and in bed under a comforter decorated with cowboy hats and horseshoes.

Jonah leaned a shoulder against the door frame. "Hey, partner."

Tanner's head shot up. "Dad!" He scrambled out of bed and hurled himself at Jonah, wrapping his arms around his waist. "What are you doing here?"

"There's a bat problem in the cabin, so your mom was kind enough to let me crash here tonight."

"Bats? Cool! You know they eat bugs and stuff, right? A lot of people hate them, but they're good for the 'vironment."

"Where'd you learn so much about bats?"

"Papa. He knows everything."

The hero worship in Tanner's eyes spiked Jonah in the chest. Would his kid ever think that about him?

Tanner raced back to his bed and grabbed a book off the small table that held a lamp. "Will you read me a story?"

Soft footsteps sounded behind him, and Jonah smelled Mallory's citrusy scent before she approached. He glanced over his shoulder.

She stood in the glow of the night-light, which

softened her face. Rosie sat at her side. He longed to reach out and touch her skin. Instead, he jerked his head toward the bedroom. "Mind if I read to him?"

She shook her head. "Mind if I stay?"

"Of course not."

Jonah crossed the room and patted the bed. "Okay, buddy. Get in bed and hand me your book."

Tanner did as he was told, and Mallory stepped inside the room. She pressed her back against the wall and slid until she sat on the carpeted floor a good eight feet from them. She curled an arm around Rosie.

Settling on the bed next to Tanner, Jonah opened to the first page and started reading about a dragon named Burt. After he finished the story, he set the book on the nightstand, pulled the blankets over Tanner and then kissed his forehead. "Good night, son."

Would he ever get tired of saying that?

Never.

Only just leaving to go to his own place.

"Wait. We have to pray." Tanner held a hand out to Mallory. "Come on, Mom. Take my hand like you always do."

Mallory pushed to her feet and rounded the bed and sat on the opposite side of Tanner. She folded his small hand in hers. Then he stretched his hand out to Jonah, who copied Mallory's movements.

"Dear God, thank you for my family. Thank you for giving me a dad. Thank you for this house. Help Papa and Nana to be able to sleep tonight without me being there. In Jesus's name, amen."

The simple, innocent prayer caused Jonah's throat to thicken.

They kissed Tanner good-night, then he headed out the door and down the stairs. Jonah stood in front of the living room window, hands in his pockets, as he stared into the darkness while Mallory finished tucking their son in for the night.

"Thank you."

He turned and found Mallory standing on the bottom step, her fingers covering the wooden ball of the carved handrail. "For reading to him. You made his night. He was worried about sleeping away from the ranch tonight. Worried my parents wouldn't be able to sleep without him being there."

A smile tugged at her lips as she lowered her gaze.

He moved toward her. "He's such a great kid, Mal. You're an amazing mom. Thank you for opening the door. I know I don't deserve it. I'm just going to keep proving I've changed so I don't have to walk back out again. Someday."

Mallory held up a hand. "One day at a time. Okay? Please don't pressure me. Keep showing up for Tanner, and we'll see how the rest goes."

He shoved his hands in his pockets again and nodded.

He'd definitely keep showing up. He'd up his game and be the kind of dad his son deserved. And prove his worth to Mallory—whatever it took.

Chapter Five

What had Mallory gotten herself into?

Maybe she should've done more research before agreeing to house-sit for the next sixty days, because she knew nothing about running a fruit farm.

Especially at the beginning of the strawberry season.

Growing up on the ranch was so different.

At least Bri and Cam had gotten the beds replanted where needed, so they didn't have to worry about that. Plus, as Bri was quick to remind her, she was only a phone call away. And Jonah had several years of farming experience, so she didn't have to handle the problem on her own.

Knowing that should've eased the heaviness in her chest, but for some reason, anxiety was an unwelcome visitor this morning. Even Rosie's presence did little to ease her apprehension.

Was it because she woke up to laughter in the kitchen? Instead of leaving at first light like he'd claimed, Jonah had fixed pancakes for Tanner, definitely making the kid's day.

She loved seeing her son happy, and if having a dad did that for him, then she was thankful for Jonah's presence. Hopefully, his promises would hold, and he wouldn't bail on his son. Tanner didn't deserve that kind of heartache.

As for her and her future as Jonah's wife, she struggled with picking up the phone and calling Aaron Brewster, her family's attorney, to change her marital status. Her family's many conversations about second chances stayed with her.

Was she being reckless by giving Jonah a chance to prove himself?

With Rosie keeping up with her, Mallory followed Jonah and Tanner to the greenhouse, where Bri and Cam had started seeds for the vegetable gardens.

Morning sunshine melted the frost on the grass, but a chill hung in the air, cooling her cheeks. She zipped up her white down jacket a little higher and buried her bare hands in her pockets.

When Jonah reappeared at their door that morning wearing clean jeans and a gray hoodie, Tanner raced back upstairs and returned wearing a matching one over his Spider-Man T-shirt.

Two weeks in and he wanted to be like his dad already.

Rosie sniffed the ground while Tanner held Jonah's hand and asked a million questions.

Jonah took it in stride, giving patient and thorough answers their son would understand.

Their son.

She still struggled to wrap her head around the fact that she was no longer a single parent. She wasn't sure how she felt about including someone else in the life of the most important person in the world to her.

But she'd promised to give him a chance and wouldn't go back on her word.

Jonah held the door for her, and she stepped inside the greenhouse. A welcome respite from the wind.

Mallory walked between the long tables lined with seedlings, her fingers trailing along the surface as she took in row upon row of tiny green sprouts shooting up from the soil.

Even though the outside temps wavered around forty-five degrees, the humid air inside the greenhouse created a solid growing environment.

Rosie darted between Mallory's feet. She tried to sidestep the dog and stumbled. She pitched forward, and her cheek rammed against Jonah's back. She reached out and grabbed his thick arms to steady herself.

Where had those muscles come from?

He turned quickly and reached for her. "Falling for me already? Had I known the greenhouse would've done the trick, I would've brought you in here sooner."

His eyes lit up as a smile tugged on his lips.

"You wish." Heat warmed her face as she righted herself and released his arms.

He lowered his mouth next to her ear. "Oh, I do."

She took a step back, disliking the way her heart rate quickened. Folding her arms over her chest, she nodded toward the tables. "How long will these seeds remain in here?"

"Depending on the frost schedule, we may begin planting as early as next month. Otherwise, some of them will go in the ground in May. Until then, they can get a head start in here."

"No wonder Bri felt overwhelmed. How will we get all of this done ourselves? I still have to work at the animal shelter." Mallory's chest tightened as her fingers rolled into fists under her arms.

Rosie leaned against Mallory's right leg. She ran her fingers through the dog's silky fur. Rosie licked her fingers.

Jonah waved a hand over the seedlings. "You're having second thoughts? You seem worried. Anxious, maybe?"

"I'm fine." Her voice squeaked, and Rosie edged closer.

Jonah moved in front of her and tilted up her

chin. "If we are going to be partners, you need to be straight with me. What's going on?"

Mallory's jaw tightened. Tears pricking the backs of her eyes, she pulled in a deep breath and released it slowly, willing her pulse to return to its normal rhythm. "I'm afraid of failing. Of letting down Bri and Cam. Of not being able to provide for Tanner."

"Mallory..." Jonah's voice, low and deep, softened. "What you're feeling is valid. But you're not doing this alone. I know I haven't been there for you in the past, but I'm here now. And I'm not going anywhere. If we do fail, which I don't expect that to happen, then we do it together, regroup and set ourselves up for success."

She looked at him and scoured his face. His blue eyes sparkled with a peace that she envied. "How can you be sure?"

He pointed to the sky. "Because the Lord is with us."

The confidence in his voice tugged at her. Why couldn't she have the same positive attitude? Where was her faith?

"My dad would've said the same thing."

"Believe me—there was a time when I wouldn't have focused on faith over my fear, but the past couple of years have taught me differently." He ran a hand over Rosie's shiny coat. "She's not just a pet, is she? She calms your anxieties."

"Why do you say that?"

"Because I watched your jaw clench, hands tighten and your eyes fill with tears. Rosie seemed to have sensed it as well and leaned against your leg. As soon as you touched her, your body relaxed."

"You're too perceptive." She picked up Rosie and buried her face in the dog's neck.

He ran a finger along Mallory's jaw. "Don't try to hide it, Mal."

Heat scalded her face. Apparently, she wasn't doing a very good job of it.

"Mom has nightmares. She yells out in her sleep." Tanner looked at his dad, his expression calm, as if he'd stated the weather.

Mallory's face burned as her eyes locked with Jonah's. His expression softened. She turned away from him, not needing—or wanting—his pity. She waved a hand over the plants. "Looks like I need a crash course in farming. In the meantime, Bri gave me the admin logins for the farm site and social media channels. I can start creating posts to generate some buzz about the upcoming season."

"Mallory."

"What do you think about having a strawberry festival? Bri's grandparents used to have one every year when we were kids. After her grandpa died, Bri's family didn't have the energy to continue them. We could resurrect it again.

Just do a day thing. Maybe it would stir up some excitement and bring in more customers for the new season."

Jonah whispered something to Tanner. He nodded and raced back to the house. Then Jonah straightened and faced Mallory. "Tell me about these nightmares."

Pressing her cool hands against her hot cheeks, she leaned against one of the tables. She didn't want to utter a word, because reliving the experience in her dreams was hard enough. But the soothing tone in Jonah's voice had her longing to spill so she wasn't the only one carrying this burden.

She cupped her elbows and looked at him. "About a month before I was due to be discharged, one of my friends went through a bad breakup and needed a place to crash for a few days. I'd just returned from the pediatrician with Tanner—he had an ear infection and a fever. I gave him some meds and put him to bed. He was out. Someone knocked on the door, and when I unlocked it, this drunken loudmouth jerk pushed his way in, waving a Beretta, and demanded to know where my friend was." Mallory dropped her gaze to her feet at the painful memories. A chill shot through her. "I tried to tell him she wasn't home, but he didn't believe me at first. He kept his weapon trained on me while he searched the rooms. Tanner woke up from the yelling and started crying. Stacie's ex held us hostage and threatened Tanner if I didn't call Stacie and get her to come back."

"Mal." Jonah reached for her, but she stiffened, and he dropped his hand. "I'm sorry."

"I called her and managed to drop a code word into our conversation. She called the police. They arrived before she did. He was arrested."

"I'm so glad you were safe."

Her head jerked up. "Safe? I was hardly safe. Never in my life had I felt so unsafe, so unprotected, so powerless. My little boy's life was in danger because of a stupid choice I'd made of letting my friend stay with me." Her eyes burned, and she dashed away a tear. "For weeks, I feared going to sleep because that monster invaded my dreams. When I came home, my parents helped me find a counselor. She suggested a psychiatric service animal and was sure I'd qualify through a program for veterans with PTSD. But I refused."

"Why?"

"Because it's not debilitating. I can live my life. There are other veterans with greater needs who qualify more than I would. A few months ago, I started working at the animal shelter. One of the ladies in my parents' church had passed away, and her family surrendered Rosie. We bonded right away. I meet with a counselor every other week and have a senior dog who brings me comfort. All I want is to feel protected again."

"Why not adopt a larger dog, like a German shepherd, to help you feel safe?"

"Rosie has learned my triggers and forces me to change my focus from my anxiety to her. Her nuzzles help my heart rate to calm and my breathing to normalize. Irene, who owns the animal shelter, allows me to take her to work. I order groceries online and pay extra to have them delivered. I do my banking online—except for the discussion with the loan officer. I go to the diner, hang out at the ranch, and avoid places where I don't feel safe. I don't expect anyone to understand."

"It's nobody's business but yours. However, you may be surprised by the number of people who do understand." He waved a hand over the property. "You feel safe here?"

She nodded. "Growing up, Wallen Farm was my second home. And with the ranch nearby, I know my family could be here within minutes."

Jonah took a step toward her and lifted a hand to her face. "What do you need to feel safe? For the nightmares to stop?"

She closed her eyes and allowed herself to lean into his tender touch. Then she shook her head. "I don't know."

"Mom! Dad! Come quick!"

Mallory's eyes flew open and found Tanner running toward the greenhouse. His cheeks were pink from the cold. "What's the matter?"

"You gotta save it." Without another word, he charged across the yard.

Jonah hurried after him. Mallory followed them down the dirt road and across the driveway, and stopped at the fence lining the small creek that cut through the property.

Eyes wide, Tanner pointed down at the shallow creek bed. "Look! A puppy!"

"Stay here with Rosie." Mallory climbed over the fence and trailed after Jonah as he scaled the bank, splashed through the water, and scooped up the soaked and shivering animal.

He glanced at her with a dark look in his eyes. "We need to get her dried off and warmed up, then call the vet to see if we can get her checked out."

She held out her arms. "Hand her to me. You don't need to slip on those wet rocks."

He flashed a grin. "Worried about me?"

"More like worried about that baby in your arms." Mallory made a face, then unzipped her jacket.

Jonah passed her the dog, who bared her teeth at Mallory as she tried to tuck her into the warmth of her jacket.

Mallory took in the dog's apple-shaped face, large eyes and pointy ears—all the markings of a Chihuahua.

"Hey, it's going to be okay. You're safe now. We won't let anyone hurt you again." Mallory cradled the pup against her chest, not caring about her sweatshirt getting soaked.

Jonah climbed up the bank and back over the fence, then held out his hands. "Give her to me so you can get back up here."

She passed the dog back to him and took her turn over the fence.

Tanner peered at the soaked ball of fur. "Can we keep her?"

She sighed, her heart melting at the pathetic-looking creature, who had most likely been dropped off at the farm.

Why were people so heartless and cruel?

She looked at Jonah, and he raised an eyebrow. "You did mention you wanted to adopt dogs to help people with trauma…"

"Dogs, yes. Senior dogs who need a forever home. Not a puppy."

"But, Mom, look at her. She doesn't have a family and needs us to take care of her."

Her son was right—she did need care.

Reclaiming the dog and putting her back inside her jacket, Mallory heaved a sigh. "Okay, but first we need to call the vet and see if the dog is chipped. Maybe someone lost her and they're looking for her."

For some reason, Mallory doubted it, but she didn't want her son to get his hopes up if the dog belonged to someone else and had gotten lost.

Tanner whooped and thrust a fist in the air.

The puppy burrowed deeper into her arms. "You two have to help. I don't want to care for a puppy on my own."

"We promise." Their voices melded together.

Tanner ran ahead and waved an arm. "Come on, Dad. Let's go find a place for her to sleep. I think she's tired. Maybe she can sleep in my room."

Mallory trailed behind them, remembering the towers of boxes still needing to be unboxed, seeds needing to be planted, farming information to be learned, a festival to organize and now a puppy depending on her. On them.

Somehow, they'd make it work. Even if it meant relying on Jonah more than she'd wanted.

Jonah had been an idiot all those years ago.

He'd been labeled a "screw-up" too many times in the past and thought leaving Mallory was the best thing for her. But he wasn't being unselfish by letting her out of a relationship with a man who wouldn't amount to much.

In reality, he ran from commitment just as his mother had done.

His own selfishness and insecurities left his wife on her own. If he'd been the husband she deserved, then he could've protected her and Tanner from the abusive boyfriend who broke into her apartment. Or if he'd been around, maybe the friend wouldn't have asked Mallory for a place to stay.

He couldn't change the past, and dwelling on his mistakes did nothing but twist up his insides.

He shifted the puppy in his hand and continued feeding her from the tiny bottle Mallory had gotten from her parents.

After they'd returned to the farmhouse and wrapped the pup in a blanket, Mallory called the vet her family's ranch used. Even though he was a large-animal veterinarian, Dr. Brown stopped by and gave the dog a thorough exam. He figured she was about six weeks old and agreed with Mallory that someone had probably abandoned it. He rattled off a list of what the animal would need. While Mallory gave the puppy a bath, Jonah ran to the feedstore and bought supplies to care for her.

Since his return, Tanner had been bouncing through the house like it was Christmas morning, eager to play with the shy canine.

Jonah glanced at Mallory. "You okay?"

Mallory took the puppy from him and then waved a hand over the stacks of boxes lining the wall next to the staircase. "I'm not even unpacked, and now I need to find a place for this little one to sleep tonight."

"We'll make it work, Mal."

She eyed him. Was that a look of disbelief on her face? To be honest, he wasn't sure what "making it work" would look like, but he would do what he could to follow through on his word.

She turned to Tanner. "You found her. What would you like to name her?"

His eyes widened as his attention stayed on the puppy, but that didn't stop the smile from spreading across his face. A smile that filled Jonah with joy every time he saw it. He never wanted his son to have anything other than that same look of pure joy on his face.

Tanner looked at Mallory. "I don't know. Mom, what do you think?"

Mallory ran a hand over his head. "You were her hero by letting us know you found her. You saved her, so you get to name her."

"Names are important. I don't want to make a mistake."

She tapped his chest. "When it comes from the heart, it's not a mistake."

If only she believed her own words.

Tanner cupped his hand around the small pup's brown-and-white face. "I like Buddy, because I know how it makes me feel when you and Dad call me 'Buddy.' But she's a girl."

Jonah slung an arm over his son's narrow shoulders. "Buddy's a great name. She's also a fighter, with the way she didn't get swept downstream. I have a good feeling about her. She wasn't ready to give up, and now she deserves a second chance. What about Rebel?"

"But isn't being a rebel a bad thing?"

"It depends on your circumstances. You can rebel against something that's wrong and want to fix it in the right way. But if you're rebelling against the right rules, then that's where you can get into trouble. This little girl is rebelling against her situation. She wants more than what her previous owners gave her, and it can remind us to give others a second chance." He didn't dare look at Mallory, but he could feel her eyes boring into him.

"I like Rebel, but I don't know." Tanner moved in front of Mallory. "What do you think, Mom?"

Mallory ran a finger over the little dog's short hair, now warm and dry after the bath. "She's tiny and has a fighting chance, thanks to you. She's a cuddler, like you used to be when you were born." She paused and ruffled Tanner's hair.

"Mom…" He glanced at Jonah as he tried to smooth down his hair. "I'm not a baby anymore."

"Tanner, no matter how old you get, you will always be my baby." She winked at their son, then returned her focus to the dog. "What about Hope?"

"Hope? Why that name?"

"Because growing up, Papa always reminded us to hold on to hope—no matter what was happening in our lives. If we put our trust in God, then He would see us through any situation.

Naming her Hope can help someone else to learn to trust."

Tanner grinned. "It's a girlie name."

"Of course it's a girlie name—she's a girl."

"She's tiny. How will she keep up with us?"

"Once she's healthy and strong, maybe we'll have to keep up with her. Otherwise, we'll slow down for her."

"Hope's a good name." Jonah drew Tanner against his side. "We guys need a steady female influence to keep us grounded."

Tanner turned and looked at him with a scrunched-up face. "Grounded? Like we're in trouble? I didn't do anything wrong."

Jonah laughed. "Not that kind of grounded. Grounded as in helping us do what we're supposed to by being a positive influence, reminding us to take things at the right pace and not run ahead. Just slow down and make the right choices."

Tanner wrinkled his nose. "I don't know. That sounds boring. I like Hope."

Mallory smiled.

Did she realize how much her face lit up every time she did that?

Jonah's lower back burned. He stood and glanced at his watch. "I need to get the cabin cleaned up so I can crash there tonight."

"Why do you have to go? Why can't you stay here in the house with us? Like other mommies and daddies? Nana and Papa are married, and they don't live in different houses. Same with Aunt Macey and Uncle Cole. Uncle Bear and Aunt Piper have the same house too. Uncle Wyatt and Aunt Callie just got married. They don't have different houses." Tanner's bottom lip popped out as he crossed his arms over his chest, tears shimmering in his eyes. "Why do we have to be different? Why can't we be the same?"

Mallory's cheeks darkened, and Jonah's chest tightened as he knelt in front of Tanner. He placed a hand on his son's shoulders. "Remember a couple weeks ago when your mom told you about me?"

Tanner nodded, sniffing. "Yes, God answered my prayers for a dad. I thank Him every day."

Jonah swallowed, glanced at Mallory and then looked back at his son. "Sometimes grown-ups make mistakes, and I made a big one."

"Well, if you make a mistake, then just say you're sorry. Mom will forgive you. That's what she tells me. She said there's nothing that I can do that she won't forgive. She says it's better to tell the truth and to say you're sorry."

Once again, out of the mouths of babes.

"I agree with your mom. Problem is, sometimes those really big mistakes still hurt the ones we love and care about. Even if they do forgive, it takes time to trust again. I want to give your mom time to trust me again."

Tanner shook his head. "One time I heard Papa tell Nana he was sorry for the mistake he made, and he kissed her and she said, 'I forgive you.'" He turned to Mallory. "Why can't you do that, Mom? Give Dad a kiss and tell him it'll be all better?"

Mallory's wide eyes volleyed between him and their son. "Excuse me, I need to take care of something." She hurried out of the room with Hope still in her arms and Rosie at her feet, but not before Jonah caught the tear sliding down her cheek.

He released a sigh. "Tanner, my man, no matter what happens between your mom and me, that does not change how we feel about you. Ever. Always remember that."

Tanner nodded, his face downcast as he glanced at Mallory's empty chair. "Mom said the same thing. What did you do that was so bad? You must've gotten in big trouble, because Mom always forgives me right away."

Even as the pain spiked his chest, Jonah couldn't hold back a chuckle. "You're a pretty awesome kid. You know that?"

"I do, because Nana and Papa tell me, and I always believe them."

"That's a good choice. They won't steer you wrong. Let's get Hope's bed ready so she can get some rest after a hard morning."

"Where is she going to sleep?"

Jonah paused. "Very good question."

"Can she sleep in my room?"

"We need to ask your mom."

"But you're my dad. Can't you tell me if it's okay or not?"

"I could, but I still want to make sure your mom is on board with it since we're a team. A team works together, especially when there's a terrific kid and an adorable pup to look out for."

He turned toward the living room and found Mallory standing in the doorway, hands in her pockets. "I put the crate in front of the fireplace. We can decide where Hope will sleep later. I need to make some lunch for Tanner. Would you like to stay and eat with us?"

"You sure?"

She nodded.

"Okay, yeah. I'd like that. Thanks. I'd like to talk with you more about a CSA."

She moved into the kitchen and removed a loaf of bread from a basket on the counter. "What was that again?"

"Community supported agriculture. Essentially, our customers would buy shares into the upcoming harvest, then receive their portion of the variety of fruits and vegetables we'll be offering. If we decide to do that, then we could create a sign-up for our website and share about it on social media."

"I'm not against the idea, but I would like to learn more about it."

"Understandable. We can talk more over lunch. I can share what I know, then give you more resources to check out so you can make an informed decision."

Maybe if she could learn to trust him with matters regarding the farm, then she'd see that all he wanted was to protect her heart.

One thing at a time.

Chapter Six

Even though he'd been born and raised in Colorado, Shelby Lake, the lakeside community in Northwestern Pennsylvania shadowed by the Allegheny Mountains, had felt more like home the past few years.

Jonah had planned to return to the Mid-Atlantic state once he'd made amends with his dad and cousin, but learning he had a son had changed all that.

But FaceTiming with Micah and Paige Holland, the owners of A Hand Up, the transitional home for disabled veterans, made him long for the Holland farm, where he'd found his peace and learned how to move from surviving to thriving.

"Hey, man. Truth be told, you about knocked me over with your text. A kid. That's great." Micah leaned back in the chair and cradled his own son, who was wrapped in a blanket.

"Yeah, Tanner's incredible. I'm so blessed. I just wish I hadn't left Mal and could've been there for them."

"Remember Dad's favorite phrase? You can't change the past—"

"You can learn from it and not make the same mistakes." Jonah pointed to Micah's son, then to his own forehead. "Fatherhood looks good on you. Smooths out some of those wrinkles."

Micah settled the baby closer to his chest. "Having only one arm, I'm always worried about dropping him. But by the grace of God, I've got a steady grip on him."

"Hey, I wanted to ask you a personal question, if you don't mind."

"Shoot."

"When I arrived at A Hand Up, you mentioned you had nightmares from your accident."

"Yeah, tore me up at night and left me dragging the next day. Dealing with something pretty heavy?"

Jonah paused. "No…not me. I learned someone close to me is dealing with nightmares. I want to help he—the…friend, but I don't know how."

Micah leaned forward, eyebrow raised. "Does this 'friend' partner with you on the farm?"

"I can't betray a confidence. You understand."

"Absolutely. More than you know."

Paige came into view of the webcam, waved to Jonah and then took the baby from Micah. After she moved out of view of the camera, Micah rubbed a hand over his close beard that hid his scars. "Pray for your friend. Encourage them to seek professional guidance."

"I am, and she is—I mean, *my friend* sees a counselor."

"Good. Be supportive, but don't pressure the friend to talk. When he or she is ready, then listen. Ask your friend to recount the nightmare. Remind her—or him—what is real and what isn't. Sometimes talking about the emotions that cause the nightmares helps too. Stress and anxiety can be common triggers, so do what you can to ease some of those, if you're aware of what they are."

"Yeah, that's the thing—I don't really know what they are. And I don't want to be the cause of more anxiety for this person."

"Then maybe you shouldn't talk about me behind my back."

Jonah looked up and found Mallory standing in the doorway with her arms crossed over her chest, her jaw set and her eyes filled with fire.

Oh, man.

Jonah jerked his attention back to his phone. "Hey, brother. I gotta go. I'll call you later."

Micah lifted his chin. "Talk to you soon. I'd say good luck, but we know that doesn't exist. Besides, it seems like you need more than that."

Yeah, Jonah didn't believe in luck. But he wouldn't mind a hefty dose of Divine Intervention to help him out of this hole he'd just dug.

He set his phone down and stood, wiping his palms on his jeans. Then he held up a hand. "Listen, Mal, it's not what you think."

"No, you listen." She strode toward him and poked his chest. "Just when I think you've changed, you betray my confidence. How could you do that?"

He grabbed her hand and wrapped his fingers around hers. "I didn't betray anything. I want to help, so I asked my buddy Micah how he overcame his nightmares. I didn't mention your name or anything about you. I kept it general."

She pulled her hand away and turned her back to him, shaking her head. Then she whirled back around. "How can I learn to trust you with the big stuff if you can't handle the small stuff?"

Jonah ground his jaw. "I've done everything I can over the past few weeks to show you can trust me with the big stuff and the small stuff. These nightmares—those aren't small things. I know what they're like. After I was injured, I used to relive the blast over and over again. I'd wake up slicked in sweat with my heart pounding and my lungs on fire. They're causing you pain, and that eats me up. I hate knowing it's one more thing you have to deal with because I wasn't there for you."

"Get over yourself, pal. I can handle this. I don't need you fixing me."

"I didn't say I was trying to fix you, so stop twisting my words."

"Fine. I don't have time for this anyway. I stopped by to let you know one of Aunt Lynetta's servers went home sick, and she asked me to help cover the dinner rush. Tanner's still at the ranch. I was going to suggest you two come to the diner and have dinner, but now I'm not so sure it's a good idea."

He hooked his thumbs through his belt loops. "I think it's a great idea. I can pick up Tanner and take him into town."

Mallory shook her head. "No, my mom will drop him off, then he can hang out until I'm done."

"You don't trust me to drive our son ten minutes into town."

Mallory opened her mouth, then closed it. Her shoulders lifted as she pulled in a breath and blew it out. "I'm trying. I am. Even if it doesn't seem like it. Tanner's been the most important person in my life since the two pink lines appeared on the test stick. I live in this constant fear of something happening to him."

Jonah touched her cheek, then lifted her chin. "I get it. I do. Until a few weeks ago, I didn't know he was alive. Now that I do, I want to wrap the kid in Bubble Wrap so nothing happens to him." He waved a finger between them. "We've seen too much, experienced too much, and it's challenged our perspectives. But we need to learn to trust God…and each other…to do what's best for Tanner. If it gives you more peace of mind to have your mom meet me at the diner, then fine. I don't want to be the cause of more anxiety for you."

She looked at him with shimmering eyes. "Thank you. I'm sorry for being such a freak. I am trying to change."

Jonah frowned. "Freak? Oh, no. You are not allowed to call yourself names. Having anxiety is challenging in many ways, but you are not a freak. Promise me that's the last time you say that."

She nodded. "You're right. Sometimes, it seems easier to put myself down before others can." Then she cupped his face and brushed her lips across his cheek. "I'm sorry for overreacting. I'll call my mom and let her know you're picking up Tanner."

Jonah was afraid to move, afraid to break the fragile strands of hope that threaded them together at that moment. Part of him felt like a thirteen-year-old not wanting to wash his cheek because the cute girl in class had kissed him.

He cleared his throat and nodded. "You do what you feel is best, and I'll go along with it."

Mallory looked at him a moment, then reached for the doorknob. "What I think is best is to learn how to compromise. You can't be the only one changing in this relationship. I need to do my part too."

Without another word, she opened the screen door and stepped onto the porch, closing it quietly behind her.

He wanted to chase after her, to ask what she meant by *relationship*, but again, he remained rooted as fresh hope surged through him.

Maybe staying in Colorado could feel like home after all.

Mallory hadn't waited tables in a while, but apparently it was like riding a bike. From the moment she tied the *Netta's Diner* apron around her waist and approached her first table, the years of serving customers after school and on Saturdays came back to her.

She reached for two warm plates off the pass bar, and the scent of sizzling fries made her stomach growl. She carried the clubs and fries to the last booth and set the plates in front of a couple who attended her church. "There you go, Bruce and Tanya. Can I get you anything else?"

Bruce lifted his nearly empty cup. "I wouldn't say no to more coffee."

She shot him a smile. "You got it."

She returned to the prep area behind the breakfast bar and grabbed the freshly brewed pot. As she returned to the booth, the front door opened, bringing in a blast of chilly early-evening air.

Loud laughter and deep male voices filled the diner as a group of guys paraded through the door and filled the two four-top tables pushed together in the middle of the dining room.

Most of them appeared to be in their early to midtwenties and dressed in cargo shorts, different colored hoodies and wearing backward ball caps displaying different sports teams.

One of the men turned over his white coffee mug and lifted it. "Hey, sweetheart, mind filling up my cup?" His loud, slurred voice indicated he'd been drinking something stronger. He gave her a grin that looked like a leer.

Mallory tightened her hold on the coffeepot handle so she wouldn't pour it over his oversize head. Accidentally, of course.

She forced a smile and did as he'd asked. "Good evening. My name's Mallory, and I'll be your server. Would anyone else like coffee?"

One of the guys sitting in the middle of the combined tables lifted his mug and gave her what he probably hoped was a sexy smile. "I would, unless you're offering something else?"

She filled his cup and forced her face not to scrunch up due to the odor of alcohol soaking his breath.

Great, just what she needed—a tableful of half-drunk loudmouths with more attitude than common sense.

As she took the rest of the drink orders, the

bells jingled against the glass door. She looked up as Tanner skipped into the diner, followed by Jonah.

Her heart knocked against her rib cage.

Seriously?

Tanner gave her a little wave, then raced to the kitchen, most likely trying to find Aunt Lynetta or to give Uncle Pete a hug.

She jerked her head toward one of the empty booths lining the wall by the window.

Jonah slid into the seat so he could face the door.

She tucked her order pad into the pocket of her apron, then headed over to him as he turned his mug over and moved it closer to her coffeepot.

"Looks like you've been pretty busy."

She focused her attention on pouring coffee without splashing and nodded.

Jonah peered around her. "I'm not sure what Tanner wants to drink."

"Chocolate milk. Every time he comes in, Aunt Lynetta makes it special for him and adds a little whipped cream."

"And you're okay with that?"

She lifted a shoulder. "I don't mind it occasionally. Uncle Pete and Aunt Lynetta don't have kids of their own, so Tanner and my nieces and nephew are kind of like their surrogate grandkids."

"It's great they're so well loved."

"Yes, it is. I'll chase Tanner out of the kitchen and grab drinks for my middle table, then I'll come back and get your orders."

"Take your time. We're not going anywhere."

That's what she was afraid of.

Less than five minutes later, she'd sent Tanner to Jonah's booth, then balanced a tray of soft drinks as she headed for her rowdy table.

As she set an ice-cold Diet Pepsi in front of a dark-haired guy who didn't look old enough to shave, let alone drink, he reached for her hand. "What'd you say your name was again, sweetheart? Or should I just call you mine?"

While his buddies nearly bust a gut, she stepped out of his reach and leveled him with a glare. "Seriously? Does that line ever work for you? My name's Mallory, not *sweetheart*. Touch me again, and I will be forced to take appropriate action."

Jonah slid out of his booth and stood next to her, feet apart and hands balled up at his sides. "Problem, Mal?"

"Nothing I can't handle, right?" Raising an eyebrow, she looked at Mr. Touchy Feely.

The guy mumbled something as his face turned as red as his T-shirt. His buddies laughed and elbowed him. The guy across from him jerked his chin toward Jonah. "Hey, Pops. Have a seat. We've got everything under control."

"Pops?" Jonah made a face and held out his hands. "Dude."

"Yeah, Pops. You act like you're her dad or something."

Jonah pressed a hand against Mallory's back. "Try her husband."

The guy's eyes narrowed as he stared at Mallory's left hand. "I don't see no ring."

"And I don't see much common sense at this table, but that doesn't mean you don't have any… or maybe you don't." Jonah drew back his shoulders, which emphasized his broad chest—not that she was paying attention or anything. "This is a family diner. How about you keep it clean and enjoy your meal so everyone else can do the same?"

The drunk guy pushed to his feet, his chair skidding against the booth behind him. "Or what are you going to do about it?"

Aunt Lynetta rounded the breakfast counter, a towel still in her hand. She strode over to the end of the table. "Hey, guys. Drinks are on the house. How about you find some other place to eat? You're not allowed to hassle my servers."

"And who are you, Grandma?"

"I own the joint. Now leave before I call the police and have you arrested for harassment."

Chairs scraped against the tile floor as the jerks hauled themselves away from the table. They shot dirty looks toward Mallory and Jonah, who still had his hand pressed against Mallory's lower back.

Once they left, she darted a look at her aunt. "Sorry."

"For what? You're not responsible for their actions."

As Mallory cleared half-finished coffee cups and torn sugar packets and mopped up spilled drinks, her insides trembled. Why had she agreed to fill in? She was better off working at the shelter, where the animals didn't judge or harass her.

She filled her tray and passed by Bruce and Tanya's booth. She reached for their stack of empty plates. "Sorry for the commotion. Would you like some dessert?"

Tanya put her hand on Mallory's arm. "I'm too full, but I wanted to say I liked how you handled them. You're gutsy."

Gutsy. Huh.

"Thank you, Tanya. I'll get your check."

Aunt Lynetta took the stack of plates from Mallory. "Bruce, how about a piece of apple pie? On the house? I just pulled it from the oven."

"Lynetta, that's so sweet of you, but I couldn't eat another bite. Pete's a fine cook."

"How about I box up a couple of pieces for you to enjoy later?"

Mallory followed her aunt into the kitchen. "I'll pay for their pies."

Aunt Lynetta took the tray from her and started

sorting the trash from the mugs at the dish pit. "You'll do no such thing. You are not to blame for those idiots, who would shame their mamas with their behavior. Don't accept responsibility for something that's not your fault."

Sudden tears pricked the backs of Mallory's eyes. "I should've let it go. Now you've lost sales."

"I'd rather lose sales than have my niece harassed. Your well-being is more important than anything else."

"Thank you."

"Mallory, order's up."

"Thanks, Uncle Pete."

Mallory headed back to the galley and reached for Jonah's bacon cheeseburger and Tanner's chicken fingers. She carried them to the table and set the plates in front of them. "Here you go. Need anything else, guys?"

Jonah glanced at Tanner, then looked at her. "You okay?"

She nodded, not trusting her voice, especially at the tender tone.

"Mom, can I have a cookie for dessert? I helped Aunt Lynetta take them out of the oven."

Mallory pressed a kiss to the top of his head. "You're such a big helper. Dinner first, then a cookie."

He grinned and took a big bite of one of his chicken tenders dripping in ketchup.

Jonah pushed to his feet again and rubbed his

palms on his thighs—an action she noticed when he was feeling a little nervous. He brought his mouth close to her ear. "Listen, maybe if you did wear a ring while you helped your aunt, guys like those idiots wouldn't hit on you."

She jerked back. "So it's my fault they hit on me? Those guys were morons. Most of the people who come in here have manners. Especially the regulars."

He held up his hands as if surrendering. "Sorry, I just thought—"

"Noted." She topped off his coffee, then turned away and moved to the next booth.

Her mind slipped back to her jewelry box that held the narrow gold band she'd worn for less than a month.

Somehow that memory made her even more irritated.

Chapter Seven

Of course Mallory wouldn't be wearing a wedding ring, considering she'd thought they'd been divorced for years.

Jonah kicked himself for suggesting she wear it to avoid being harassed. His attempt to help the situation just fueled her anger. And rightfully so.

Those jerks were to blame for their actions, not her.

Just as he was the one to blame for walking away from her.

He leaned back in the chair on the front porch of the cabin, his fingers locked behind his head. The cool night air whisked across his face. A bullfrog croaked somewhere on the bank of the creek. Stars speckled the dark sky.

He could get used to evenings like this.

Except he would prefer to be sitting on the farmhouse porch with Mallory at his side.

He pushed to his feet and stretched. As he turned toward the door, a light bobbed up the hill.

Jonah reached for his phone and tapped on the flashlight.

Who was on their property?

He peered through the trees and found the living room light in the farmhouse shining brightly.

He glanced around the porch, then picked up the broom he'd used earlier to sweep the deck. Not much of a weapon, but he'd make it work if need be. "Hello?"

"Dad?"

Jonah jumped down the front steps and hurried through the trees in the direction of the light. "Tanner, what you doing out here? You should be in bed."

"It's Mom. Something's wrong. She's crying. I tried to wake her up. She yelled at me not to touch her. I didn't mean it. I was just scared." Tears choked his son's words.

Jonah reached Tanner, still dressed in his pajamas and in bare feet, and crushed him to his chest. "Are you okay? Are you hurt?"

Tanner shook his head, his hair rubbing against Jonah's T-shirt.

Jonah lifted him in his arms, protesting against the pain in his lower back. "Come on. Let's go check on your mom. Maybe she had a bad dream again."

"I was sleeping, then I heard her yell my name. That's why I went to her. Now I made her mad." He buried his face in Jonah's chest.

Jonah tightened his hold on his son. "It's okay, bud. I'm sure she didn't mean it."

They reached the farmhouse, and Tanner scrambled out of Jonah's arms. He opened the front door, and they stepped inside.

Rosie raced to greet them, and he bent over and stroked her fur. She licked his chin. Hope barked from inside her small crate near the couch.

The overhead light lit up the room. Laughter came from a sitcom playing on the TV. A lightweight blue blanket lay on the couch, but Mallory wasn't there.

"Mom? Where are you?" Tanner ran toward the kitchen.

Mallory came out of the small bathroom off the living room with a wet cloth pressed against her face. Her hair had come out of the messy bun she'd worn earlier and spilled around her shoulders.

She'd changed out of the jeans and yellow *Netta's Diner* T-shirt and into a pair of navy sweatpants and a gray *Aspen Ridge Mustangs* shirt.

Her eyes widened. "Tanner? What are you doing out of bed?" Then she frowned at Jonah. "And what are you doing here?"

Tanner raced across the room and flung his arms around her waist. He pressed his cheek against her stomach. "I'm sorry, Mom. I didn't mean to make you mad."

Her eyebrows still pulled together, Mallory

knelt in front of Tanner. "Mad? Honey, what do you mean?"

"You know, when you told me not to touch you?"

Confusion masked her face. Holding on to his hand, she moved to the couch and pulled Tanner into her lap. "Buddy, I don't know what you're talking about. Did you have a bad dream or something?"

Tanner's face twisted into a scowl, and he balled up his fists and stamped a foot against the cushion. "No, Mom. Not me. You did. You had the bad dream. You called my name. I came downstairs. I tried to wake you up, but you told me not to touch you. Then you started crying. I got scared and ran to get Dad."

Mallory's eyes shifted between Tanner and Jonah, then the color left her face. She buried her face in her hand and shook her head. "Oh, honey. I'm so sorry. I wasn't yelling at you." Then she cupped Tanner's face. "I'm not mad at you. You're right—I did have a bad dream. But that's all that it was—a dream. I'm safe. You're safe. And your dad is safe. How about if we head back to bed?"

"Can Dad tuck me in too?"

Mallory stood, avoided looking at Jonah, and held out her hand to their son. "Sure."

He had a feeling she wanted to say no, but she

wasn't about to upset Tanner any more than he was already.

Rosie charged up the steps after Mallory and Tanner while Jonah followed behind.

Hope yipped from her crate. She didn't want to be left out, but Jonah didn't want to release her without Mallory's consent. He gripped the railing and headed up the stairs.

Once Tanner was tucked into bed and said a new prayer, Mallory kissed him on the forehead. "Sleep tight. I love you."

"Love you, too, Mom. I'm glad you're not mad at me, but I don't like it when you have bad dreams."

Mallory sat on the edge of his bed and smoothed his hair off his forehead. "I know. Me neither. Talking with my counselor helps. I'm sorry I upset you."

"You're not mad that I got Dad?"

"Honey, you were scared. You did the right thing by finding a responsible adult to help you. I'm just sorry it happened. Now, get some sleep." She tucked the blankets under his chin, then brushed past Jonah and headed out of the room.

Jonah crossed the room to Tanner's bed. "You're brave. You know that? It took guts to go out in the dark like that."

Tanner's eyes widened, then he smiled. "You mean it? I didn't like the noises, but I just kept focusing on the light coming from the cabin. I knew you were home and I could count on you."

Jonah's heart slammed against his rib cage as he took Mallory's place on the bed. "And that's what makes you brave—doing something in spite of being afraid."

"Are you afraid of stuff, Dad?"

"Sure. We all are, buddy."

Jonah sat up and wrapped his arms around Jonah. "Thanks for being here. I feel better when you're around."

Jonah's chest tightened as he returned his son's hug. He covered him back up, turned off the light and headed down the stairs.

The TV had been turned off, and silence blanketed the living room. Mallory had folded up the throw that had fallen onto the floor. Instead of the overhead light brightening the room, a single lamp on the side table cast a mellow glow.

The sound of water running pulled Jonah toward the kitchen. He leaned a shoulder against the door frame. "You okay?"

With her back to him, Mallory shut off the faucet, then braced herself against the front of the sink. Slowly, she shook her head.

Jonah strode across the room, touched her arm and then turned her toward him. Mallory walked into his embrace and pressed her cheek against his chest. Arms tightening around her, he drew her close and breathed in the floral scent of her shampoo.

She released a long sigh, then pulled back. Keeping her eyes level with his chest, she cleared her throat. "So, uh, what suggestions did your friend have regarding his nightmares? I can't put Tanner in that position again. He could've gotten hurt in the dark by himself. I assumed he was still upstairs sleeping."

"He's a brave kid. And strong. He gets that from you." He tilted up her chin. "Want to tell me what happened?"

Mallory dragged a hand through her hair and moved out of his embrace, leaving his arms feeling too empty.

"Even though I thought I was fine, I think the situation at the diner may have triggered the nightmare. Earlier, when that jerk grabbed me, I froze, feeling a little powerless, even though you were right there. That's the only thing I could think of."

"Micah said stress is often his trigger."

Mallory nodded. "My counselor said the same thing. A couple of months ago, I signed up for a self-defense class, then canceled it, thinking I was overreacting. This is Aspen Ridge, after all."

"It's a great town, but it's not without its faults. Self-defense classes could be a good way for you to feel empowered instead of powerless or unprotected. I'll go with you if you want to sign back up."

Mallory shook her head, then looked at him with an expression he couldn't read. "Why are you being so nice?"

He frowned. "You're my wife. Why wouldn't I be nice?"

"But you don't have to be." She waved a hand toward the window. "We're partners. You could leave it at that."

He lifted his hands, then dropped them at his sides. "I screwed up. Now I'm doing what I can to fix what I broke between us."

Mallory rubbed a thumb and forefinger over her eyes, then wrapped her arms around her waist and glanced at him. "Since we're being honest, I know I should push you out the door. It's late, and you need your rest. But I'm afraid to go to sleep right now. I don't want to dream again. Mind staying a little while longer?"

As a smile tugged at his lips, he bridged the distance between them, lowered his voice and slid a hand over her cheek. "Not at all. I haven't had a chance to talk to you about my plans for the adaptive gardens. I could bore you to sleep with those details, if you'd like."

She waved a hand to the table. "Have a seat and bore away. Want something to drink?"

"Nah, I'm good." He pulled out a chair.

After filling a glass with water and carrying it

to the table, she sat across from him. Jonah pulled out his phone, opened his Notes app and pushed it across the table to her. He spread his fingers across the screen, enlarging the sketched image. "I drew this on my iPad, so I apologize for the size here. I did a general layout so we can create the beds in any of the areas on the farm. Since they are adaptive beds, we will want to consider building them where the gardeners would have easiest access."

"That makes sense." Mallory pointed to the screen. "I realize these are just rectangles representing the layout, but how will you build the beds and determine what will be grown?"

He pointed to a semicircle. "This represents the hoop barn. The area around it is flat and accessible from the road that leads up to my cabin. I plan to build long, boxlike elevated structures and add legs. That way, anyone who wants to garden can sit or stand and still reach the top of the bed. The seedlings in the greenhouse are nearly ready to plant."

Jonah tapped an app on his phone, then typed something. He turned the screen to Mallory. "This is what I'm talking about."

She took the device, her fingers brushing his. She brought it closer to her face and enlarged the screen. "I think we should create wide paths around the beds so whomever wants to use them has plenty of access."

"That's a great idea. We can purchase some garden tools that are easier on the hands." He made a squeezing motion with his hand. "Gardening has proven to help those with PTSD, anxiety and TBI."

"TBI?"

"Traumatic brain injury. Tending to the gardens helps people take their focus off their own problems. Plus, it releases those happy hormones we all need for a healthier mental well-being."

"Maybe that's why I've always loved this place." Mallory pushed her chair back and carried her empty glass to the sink. Then she kept one hand on the counter and faced him. "By the way, I meant to mention this at the diner, but with everything that happened, I forgot. Irene Douglas called. There's a dog she wants me to consider for adoption. The owner had to surrender her when she moved into assisted living." She wrapped her arms around her waist. "Would you want to check it out with me? I'm not working tomorrow, but we could go after dropping Tanner off at school."

He couldn't help the grin that spread across his face. "Yes, absolutely. I'll be here first thing in the morning."

"Thanks." She stifled a yawn. "I think I can sleep now."

"Is that your subtle way of kicking me out?" He pushed to his feet and pocketed his phone. "You'll be okay?"

She nodded, then lowered her gaze. "Yes, thanks. Sorry I disrupted your evening."

He strode over to the sink, lifted her chin and then reached for her upper arms. He brushed a kiss across her forehead. "Darlin', feel free to disrupt it anytime."

Without another word, he turned and headed for the front door before he did something stupid to drive her away. Like take her in his arms and give her a real kiss.

In due time.

Until then, he'd be by her side and help with whatever he could.

Mallory smelled bacon.

That wasn't good, considering she was still buried under the blankets in her bed, which was on the second floor, away from the kitchen.

Tanner knew not to cook without her present.

That meant… Jonah.

She glanced at the clock and groaned. She'd overslept. She should've been up an hour ago so she could get Tanner ready for school and out the door.

Mallory threw back the blankets, pushed her hair away from her face, and quickly changed out of her PJs and pulled on a pair of jeans and a light blue hoodie. She stuffed a pair of socks in her front pocket and hurried barefoot across the hall to the bathroom. After a quick face wash and brushing her hair into a ponytail, she hurried down the steps.

She followed the scents of bacon and fresh-brewed coffee. Jonah stood at the stove with his back to her. A dish towel hung over his left shoulder.

"Hi, Mom." Tanner looked up from his plate of half-eaten eggs and bacon. "Dad made breakfast and promised to take me to school."

"Oh, he did?"

Jonah turned and shot her a smile. "Morning."

The single word, spoken low and drawn out, sent her heart in a tumble.

She moved to the counter, reached for a mug from the cabinet above the coffee maker and filled it with delicious-smelling dark roast. She added a splash of creamer and a spoonful of sugar, then stood next to Jonah. "*You* promised to take Tanner to school?"

He placed the last piece of sizzling bacon on the paper-towel-covered plate, turned off the heat and then faced her. "What I said was, I was going with you to drop him off. I'm telling you—the kid hears only what he wants."

"Kind of like his dad." She mumbled the words against the rim of her mug, but he must've understood, because Jonah laughed softly.

"How do you want your eggs?"

"Eggs?" She glanced at the clock on the stove. "I don't have time to eat. I need to drop Tanner off at school, then head to the animal shelter, re-member?" She took another drink of coffee, then set the cup on the counter. "But first, I need to finish getting ready."

"How about this? I'll make you a breakfast sandwich that you can eat in the car, then I'll help Tanner finish up. Then we'll drop him off and go look at the dog together, as planned."

"But..."

"But what?"

Other than her family, she wasn't used to rely-ing on someone else. So Jonah's willingness still kind of threw her off.

She shook her head. "Nothing. That sounds good."

He held up a closed fist. "Partners, remem-ber?"

She hesitated a moment, then bumped his fist with her own. "Partners. Right."

The light dimmed in his eyes. "Would you rather I stayed here?"

She studied him a moment, then shifted her eyes to their son, who watched them with a smile on his face while scooping the last of his eggs into his mouth. "No, not at all. We'll go together. Why not?"

Actually, she could come up with a thousand reasons why not, but she had promised to meet Jonah halfway.

Since they'd arrived at the farm, he'd done only

what was best for her and Tanner. It was time for her to step up and ensure her son was adjusting well to the recent changes in his life. That meant she needed to spend more time with Jonah and get to know him all over again.

Fifteen minutes later, Tanner buckled himself into his booster seat. As Mallory started for the driver's side, she paused and hefted her keys in her hand. "Jonah, catch."

His arm shot up as the keys sailed across the roof of her car. He caught them in one hand.

"Why don't you drive so I can eat this sandwich?"

"Sure thing, but we can take my truck if you want me to drive."

Mallory rounded the front of the car and playfully shoved Jonah away from the passenger door. "Thanks, but I'm partial to my heated seats. And Tanner's already buckled in. Maybe next time."

"Next time, huh?"

She lifted a shoulder as she opened the door. "We'll see."

Jonah held the door open, and once she was inside, he closed it, headed for the driver's side and slid behind the wheel. His fresh scent filled the car.

Okay, maybe this was a mistake.

No *maybe* about it.

He was getting under her skin.

As if he could read her mind, he shot her a grin and started the engine.

Mallory blew out a breath, then took a bite of the egg, bacon and cheese nestled between a still-warm, toasted English muffin. "Yum. What's in this?"

"My secret ingredient."

"If you say *love*, I'm going to toss it out the window."

"I was going to say *Italian seasoning*, but *love* works too."

Mallory rolled her eyes and took another bite, savoring the flavor. She lifted the sandwich. "Thanks again, by the way."

"Any time."

And now she didn't need to be a mind reader to know he meant it.

After managing the drop-off line in front of Aspen Ridge Elementary like he'd been doing it for years, Jonah drove them to the opposite end of town.

A few minutes later, he pulled into a parking space in front of the red building with black trim. The Aspen Ridge Animal Shelter sat on several acres of the Douglas's ranch. Their white-sided two-story house with black shutters and a covered front porch sat to the left of the shelter.

"Didn't your brother date their daughter or something?"

"Yes, Linnea. They got married after Wyatt

graduated from boot camp. Sadly, Linnea passed way while giving birth to their daughter, Mia. Wyatt still calls Ray and Irene his family, and they've embraced Callie, Wyatt's new wife, quite well."

"I'm sorry for your family's loss, but I'm glad to hear Wyatt is happy again."

"Yeah, me too. He had a few rough years, but Callie is pretty great. She's adopting Mia, but that's only for legality's sake. Mia calls her 'Mom.'"

Jonah drummed his fingers on the steering wheel as he turned his head and peered at the building through the windshield. "They've updated since I was here as a kid."

Two budding dwarf apple trees sat on either side of the building. A row of evergreen shrubs lined the front. A plaster black Lab holding a welcome sign sat next to a wrought iron bench.

"Ray and Irene put a lot of work into creating an inviting environment for the animals." Mallory stuffed her napkin in the pocket of her jacket, grabbed her purse and then reached for the door handle.

But Jonah was quicker.

He opened the door and held it while she stepped onto the blacktop parking lot.

As they entered the building, the sounds of barking dogs spilled outdoors. Mallory headed for the front reception desk.

Irene Douglas, the owner, popped her head over the computer monitor. "Hi, Mallory. You're not scheduled to work today."

"No, Jonah and I came in to see the dog you mentioned." She turned to Jonah. "This is Irene Douglas, who owns the shelter. Irene, do you remember Jonah Hayes?"

"Jonah Hayes, of course. My husband, Ray, has coffee with your dad quite often. I heard you were back in town." She rounded the counter and pulled him in for a hug.

"Good to see you again, Mrs. Douglas. It's been years. I think we adopted our dog Snickers from you."

"Oh, that little rascal. I remember him. Cute pup. Looked for trouble, though."

"My dad used to say Snickers and I were two peas in a pod."

"Let me take you to Lucy. She's the sweetest thing. Just like with Rosie, her owner can no longer care for her due to health reasons." She waved for them to follow.

They headed down the hall to the glass-enclosed kennels. Different breeds pawed at the walls and barked as they passed.

Irene stopped at a corner enclosure and opened the door. A small pile of black-and-white fluff was curled up in the corner of the cot. She lifted her head and looked at Mallory with the most soulful eyes.

Mallory pressed a hand to her chest. "Oh, my heart. She is precious."

"She looks sad." Jonah stood behind her and placed his hands on her shoulders.

She looked up at him. "I'm sure she misses her owner."

"I know Judith was a bit distraught to give her up. Unfortunately, her daughter wasn't in a position to take Lucy. I nearly cried along with them as they said goodbye. I promised to find a good home for her, and you came to mind."

Mallory looked at the older woman. "Thank you for letting me know about her."

She stepped inside and crouched next to the cot. Lucy's eyes followed her every movement. "Hey, sweet girl. Can I pet you?"

Mallory held out a hand, and Lucy sniffed it. Mallory stroked the dog's back, feeling the trembling beneath her hand. "Aw, she's scared."

She pulled her hand back, but then Lucy edged closer to her. Mallory shifted into a sitting position on the floor. Lucy placed a paw on Mallory's knee. Mallory looked at Irene. "What do you know about her?"

"She's about ten years old, I believe. Judith's had her since she was a pup, which made it even harder to part with her. Lucy's a mixed breed but mostly cocker spaniel. She has an issue with her left eye, and our vet said she will need to have surgery before she can be adopted. Would you like to take her for a walk?"

Mallory pushed to her feet, then turned to Jonah. "I would. What about you?"

He stepped back and waved for her to pass in front of him. They moved back to the reception area and allowed Irene to bring Lucy to them.

As they headed out the back door, Jonah pressed a hand against Mallory's lower back. "You've already fallen in love with her, haven't you?"

A familiar lump clogged her throat, and Mallory could only nod. As they walked down the dirt road behind the shelter, Mallory held the leash loosely as she allowed Lucy to sniff the unfamiliar territory.

A warmer-than-usual spring breeze stroked her face, carrying scents of the horses and barn from the Douglas's ranch.

Lucy pulled on the leash, so Mallory wrapped it around her hand a couple of times and shortened the length. The dog paused and looked at her once more, almost as if asking for permission to explore.

"With her black legs and white feet, she looks like she's wearing socks." Jonah laughed softly, the richness of his voice flowing through her.

"Am I being ridiculous for wanting to do this?" Mallory said the words almost to herself.

"I don't think 'ridiculous' is the right word.

You have a heart for dogs. And you've been clear about your goal. Do you feel comfortable bringing a new dog into the house with Rosie and Hope?"

She shielded her eyes and looked at him. "I want to, but what if it's not the right thing to do?"

"Right for who?"

"Well, I'm still trying to acclimate Rosie to Hope, and now the poor thing will have another canine in her space. Plus, there's so much to do around the farm—Bri was right. It is a lot of work. And what if we can't stay on the farm? How will I find a place that allows three dogs?" Mallory glanced at Jonah, trying not to let the panic whirlwind in her mind to take hold. She rubbed the heel of her hand against her sternum. "Plus, what's Tanner going to think?"

Jonah reached for Mallory's upper arms and gave them a light squeeze. The kindness in his eyes eased some of the tightness in Mallory's chest. "Mal, adopting a dog and giving her a forever home with the right family is a good thing. Tanner's a dog lover, so I'm sure he won't have an issue. He's already loving on Hope. As for the farm—yes, it's good to plan ahead, but don't worry about the *what if*s. We'll deal with that when we get there. The question is, will it be too much for you with everything else going on?"

Mallory lifted her shoulder, then trailed after Lucy as she sniffed a dandelion. "I could turn

Cam's former office off the dining room into a canine play space. With the way the morning sunshine warms the room, the dogs could have their crates, beds and toys in there. They can nap and play when the weather keeps them inside. With all the space on the farm, we could create an enclosed play yard so they're safe from running into the road or into the woods."

"That sounds like a good idea. What can I do to help?"

"Make sure I'm not taking on more than I can chew."

"Partners, remember?" He rubbed a hand across his chin. "Irene said something that has me thinking."

"What's that?"

"I know you want to use the dogs to help women who've experienced trauma. But what about men and women like Judith who have to give up everything, including their beloved pets, for assisted-living care? When I was a kid, one of my friends visited nursing homes and assisted-living apartments with his mom—she had a comfort therapy dog who offered smiles and emotional wellbeing for elderly people."

Mallory pondered Jonah's words. "It's definitely something to look into. I'm sure some sort of training will be necessary."

"Your family is all about cattle and horses, yet you prefer dogs over riding."

Mallory lifted a shoulder. "I'm the family misfit."

"That's a little harsh, isn't it?"

"When I was ten, I begged my parents to allow me to do barrel racing like my friends. They signed me up for lessons with a local coach, but we didn't connect well. Her perfectionism triggered my anxiety. I felt like I couldn't measure up to her expectations and continued to make mistakes. My competitions were terrible, and I always left feeling humiliated. When I complained to my parents, they canceled my lessons. I overheard my dad say the lessons were expensive, and if I wasn't going to give it my all, then why keep paying for them. I stopped riding. My grandparents' dog just had puppies, and I fell in love with them. They didn't judge me for not living up to expectations."

"And that's why you mentioned not wanting to let Cam and Bri down with the farm."

"No one wants to feel like a failure."

"Mallory, you're far from a failure. You're an amazing mom. You're so well organized. You're quick to lend a hand when someone needs help."

"Tell that to my siblings—Bear's a bull-riding champion. Macey was rodeo queen who is in the process of opening her own childcare center. Wyatt is a horse whisperer. Everly teaches children and helps them to find success. I'm not feeling sorry for myself. I'm fine with being the very ordinary sibling."

"You have a huge heart. You're kind and compassionate. That's far from ordinary."

"My parents taught us to love well. It's one of their values, and we've embraced it. I just want to be a good mom to Tanner and offer dogs like Rosie and Lucy a loving home to live out their senior years."

"And it takes a special kind of person to do that." Jonah touched Mallory's shoulder and turned her to face him. "Let's do it—let's begin the paperwork to adopt Lucy. I'll help you with getting the canine room set up and getting her acclimated with the other dogs." He wrapped an arm around Mallory's shoulders. "We misfits have to stay together."

While she appreciated his encouraging words, part of her struggled with believing them. If she had all those same qualities that he seemed to admire, why hadn't she been enough for him to stay all those years ago?

Chapter Eight

Jonah hoped Mallory was beginning to believe him, because he meant every word.

They reached the end of the split rail fence that ran along the road and stopped. She peered up at him. "Can I ask you something?"

"Anything."

"I'm not trying to stir up trouble, but I can't help but wonder…"

Jonah placed a hand on Mallory's arm. "What? Just say it."

"If you meant what you said, then why did you leave? I mean, nothing reinforces failure more than having your husband of less than a month send divorce papers."

"Mal…" Jonah dragged a hand over his face. "That was all me, and nothing to do with you. After my mom left, I struggled, especially in my teen years. I got into trouble and was called a screw-up more than once. I guess I started believing it. I was scared of having such a good thing. I got in my head and started to freak out."

"I wish you would've told me. We could've worked it out. Together." Her words came out so quietly yet so full of pain.

"I know, and you're right. I'm the loser who chucked the best thing that'd happened to me because I was a chicken. I was the fool who destroyed our marriage and left just as my mom did—something I vowed as a kid to never do. But I did. I thought I was leaving before I could hurt you."

She mumbled something that he couldn't quite make out but it sounded pretty close to *too late*.

He took her hands. "I know this isn't the best time or place, but I am truly sorry for the pain I caused you. If I could do it all over again, I'd like to say I'd be the bigger man and stay. To be honest, the last eight years have been the hardest and the best of my life."

"That's a contradictory statement."

"Yeah, I doubt anyone else would see getting blown up as a blessing. Believe me, I didn't see it at the time. In fact, I spent years drowning my anger and self-pity in booze. I've done things I'm not proud of, things that still cause me to feel guilty and ashamed."

"Like what?"

Jonah swallowed a couple of times as he wrestled with his words. He lowered his gaze to the ground and kicked his toe against a clump of dried grass. Then he looked at her. "Let's just say I've probably broken a few of the Ten Commandments."

Her eyes searched his face. "Do I even want to know which ones?"

Heat crawled up his neck as the pain in her voice drilled into his chest. He shook his head and reached for her once again.

She took a step back and moved Lucy in front of her, creating a barrier between them.

"I'm sorry." He didn't know what else to say.

She glanced at him quickly, then looked away, but not before he caught the shimmer in her eyes. "I shouldn't have asked the question if I didn't want to know the answer."

"I'm not that guy anymore, Mallory. Meeting Micah Holland changed me. Spending the past few years in Pennsylvania shaped me into the man I am today. I'm a guy who used to take the Lord's name in vain, and now I speak His name in reverence. I don't know what He saw in me, but He redeemed me. I don't know if it took the blast of the IED to get my attention or what. Whatever it was, I'm grateful." This time, he took a step toward her and lifted her chin so he could see her beautiful eyes. "Is there any hope you can forget about the guy from the past and see me for the guy I am today?"

Slowly, she shook her head. "I can't forget, because I fell in love with that guy from your past. He was good and kind. And I loved him very much. Now I'm getting to know you all over again, but I still see those same traits of goodness and kindness."

She guided Lucy onto the dirt road, and they headed back to the shelter.

"Micah's dad—who reminds me a lot of your father, by the way—always said we can't change our pasts. We need to learn from our mistakes so we don't repeat them. And that's what I try to do every single day."

"He sounds like a wise man." To his surprise, Mallory stopped walking, lifted her hand and pressed it against his cheek. "I know you've changed, Jonah. I see the way you are with Tanner, the way you are with the dogs and the way you are with me. I'm grateful for the transformation. But I need more time. Don't give up hope."

She leaned forward and brushed a kiss across his jaw. But he turned, and her lips grazed his. He gripped her elbows and pulled her closer to him. His mouth claimed hers as he kissed her softly, cherishing being this close to her again.

Not wanting to overstep, he moved back and blew out a breath. "I'll never give up on us again. I've learned to be a patient man. Whatever it takes to trust me again… I'll wait."

She pressed her forehead against his chest, and he wrapped an arm around her. "Thank you."

They finished their walk in silence while allowing Lucy to explore the area. Once they reached the back door, Mallory crouched in front of the door. "It was so nice meeting you, Miss Lucy. I hope to see you again."

He placed a hand on her shoulder. "We're adopting her. So you will."

Maybe by his use of the plural pronoun, she'd have more confidence that he planned to stick around.

His phone vibrated in his front pocket. He dug it out and found a calendar reminder to visit his dad.

"I need to swing by Dad's place. He has some information about a local vet's organization. Mind going with me?"

She grinned. "We came in my car, remember?"

He hooked an arm around her neck and dropped a kiss on the top of her head. "Right. I'm going to give Dad a quick call and let him know I'm coming."

"I'll head inside and let Irene know that I'll… I mean, *we'll* be adopting Lucy."

As she turned and walked away, his heart buoyed. It wasn't a declaration, but switching from *I'll* to *we'll* showed promise.

He'd take it.

He called his dad, but his call went to voicemail.

He'd swing by anyway. Maybe Dad was outside and couldn't hear the phone.

Less than fifteen minutes later, Jonah pulled

into Dad's driveway. Not only was his father's Jeep parked in the open garage, but another car, a blue sedan with Texas plates, sat behind it.

Jonah parked, rounded the front of Mallory's SUV and then reached for her door handle just as she pushed it open. "I was going to get that for you."

"I'm not used to guys opening my doors."

"You've been around the wrong guys."

Her mouth twisted as if she was trying to hold back words or a smile. Then she waved him toward the front door of the house. "I'll follow you."

With Mallory less than a foot behind him, they headed for the front door. Jonah opened it, then stepped back so Mallory could enter. He closed the door behind them. "Dad?"

Music drifted from the right side of the house. Jonah jerked his head toward the living room. "He may be watching TV and missed my phone call."

They headed down the short hall that led from the foyer to the living room. Jonah stopped suddenly, and Mallory bumped into him.

His dad stood in the middle of the living room with his arms wrapped around a woman with familiar-looking red hair that was twisted up in some sort of clip.

At that moment, his dad looked up and broke away from the woman in his arms. He cleared his throat and ran a hand over the top of his head. "Jonah. I didn't see you there."

Even though Jonah heard his father's words, he didn't respond. He couldn't. His voice was somehow lodged in his throat as he stared at the woman.

Red hair he'd remember for as long as he lived. She didn't need to turn for him to know she had blue eyes and a small scar on the right side of her chin from a fall she'd taken on the ice right before his sixth birthday.

Then she turned slowly with her hands clasped in front of her. "Hello, Jonah."

He blinked as his stomach burned. His heart thundered in his ears as a chill trailed over his skin.

"Mom?"

Smiling, she nodded and walked across the room with her hands outstretched.

Instead of moving into her embrace, he turned away from the door and grabbed Mallory's hand. "Come on. Let's go."

He strode to the front door, jerked it opened and then hurried back to the car.

"Jonah, slow down."

He looked over his shoulder and found Mallory stumbling behind him. He realized he was still holding Mallory's hand and practically dragging her. Releasing his hold, he opened the passenger-side door.

Without a word, she slid onto the seat and rubbed her reddened hand. "I'm sorry. I didn't mean to hurt you. I just needed to get out of there."

He closed the door and reached the driver's side as the front door opened. His dad stepped onto the front porch, arms folded over his chest. "Jonah, a word?"

"Can't talk right now." Jonah slid behind the wheel and slammed the door shut.

His jaw tightened as he backed out of his father's driveway and headed to the farm without saying a word.

He parked, shut off the engine and handed the keys to Mallory. "Sorry for ruining our morning."

"You didn't ruin anything. Want to talk about it?"

"There's not much to say." Jonah scoffed and ran a hand through his hair. "Apparently, my parents are back together after nearly twenty years and forgot to mention it to their son."

"Want to go for a walk or something?"

"As much as I want to say yes, I don't think I'll be very good company." He opened his door and headed for hers, but once again, she beat him to it. "I'm going to start on the elevated beds and cool off. I'll be down later."

He needed to be alone and process why his mother was back in town—and had been for a while, considering she was kissing his father.

Why hadn't she bothered to contact Jonah? Maybe that was one part of her life she didn't want to pick back up. What did that mean for him staying in Aspen Ridge?

Maybe Mallory should've stayed at the farm in case Jonah wanted to talk, but when her mom invited her for lunch, she didn't have a reason to say no. Not that she really wanted to anyway.

While she loved the farm and having her own space, she missed seeing Mom, Macey and Everly on a daily basis.

Plus, her mother had offered to help Mallory with organizing the strawberry festival, and she wasn't about to turn down that offer.

With a cooling cup of coffee by her right arm and notes spread out in front of her, Mallory rested her elbow on the table and cradled her forehead in her hand. "How did the Wallens do this every year?"

"I'm sure their first one was tough, but after that, they found a rhythm. Then they became pros. And you will too." Mom moved one of Mallory's papers out of the way and set a plate of homemade chocolate chip cookies in the middle of the table. Then she pulled out a chair. "How can I help?"

Even though Mallory was full from the chicken salad Mom had prepared, she reached for a cookie. She took a bite, then studied the site she'd pulled up on her tablet. "Some of these festivals go all weekend. That feels overwhelming to me."

"Honey, start small and see if you even like doing it. Yours doesn't have to mirror the ones Herm and Greta Wallen used to host."

"I know, but those were the best."

"What did you like most about them?"

"The food, the games with prizes, picking berries."

Mom stood and moved to the kitchen counter, where she opened a drawer and took out a pen and a notepad. She returned to the table and clicked her pen, ready to write. "Okay, let's focus on those three. Pete and Lynetta just bought a new food truck. I'm sure they'd love to have it at your festival. Dad and your brothers can put together a small petting zoo and offer wagon rides. Your sisters and I can come up with activities for families. Since Callie's such a great artist, we can ask her to do face painting. You said the strawberries are thriving. Those are your main three areas."

"Thanks, Mom. That helps."

"Of course, honey." Mom leaned forward and slid a lock of hair behind Mallory's ear. "How are you doing? I miss having you here."

Mallory cupped Mom's hand and gave it a gentle squeeze. "I miss being here, too, but I like my own space. And I'm sure Everly loves having her room back. Tanner's adjusting well. He loves hanging out with Jonah."

"You know your sister didn't mind."

"Maybe not, but we started bickering over petty things. Plus, I was too restless and kept her awake too much. She needs her sleep to deal with those brilliant minds in her classroom."

"Are you still having those same dreams?"

Mallory held up a finger as she took another bite of her cookie. "Had one the other night. I woke up Tanner. He tried to wake me, and apparently, I yelled at him. He ran to get Jonah."

"How'd that make you feel?"

Mallory suppressed a smile and didn't tell Mom she sounded like her counselor. "Embarrassed, humiliated and terrified for Tanner. But Jonah was pretty great."

"Things are getting better between you two?"

"Define 'better.' I don't want to leave the state anymore, but we're far from being the perfect family."

Mom moved to the coffee maker and retrieved the pot. She refilled Mallory's cup, then her own. "No family is perfect."

"You and Dad are pretty close."

Mom laughed, the sound bouncing off the walls. "Oh, girl. We have you fooled. Dad and I aren't perfect. Far from it. We make our share of mistakes with each other and you kids. But I love him, and he loves me, so we work hard to do better. That's all any couple can do—for themselves and their children."

Popping the last of her cookie into her mouth, Mallory brushed her crumbs into her napkin, then stirred more cream and sugar into her coffee. She pondered her mother's words as she gathered her mess of notes and stacked them in a pile. Then she stood and moved behind her mother's chair and wrapped her arms around her. "I love you, Mom. I appreciate all you and Dad have done for Tanner and me."

"What a sweet thing to say. I love you too. You know we'll do whatever we can to help you."

"I know. I'm sorry I didn't tell you about Jonah."

"You had your reasons." Mom turned in her chair. "I promised myself I'd never get involved in my kids' marriages. A lesson I learned from Grandma and Grandpa. But I will admit, I worry about you. Are you happy, Mal?"

"Happy? That's a little subjective, I think." Mallory shoved her hands in her back pockets and then moved to the window. With her nieces in school, the backyard remained quiet. She turned back to Mom. "I'm not unhappy. I'm enjoying the farm. I like adding my own touches to the farmhouse. I love the dogs. Jonah and I are getting along better. Does that make me happy?"

"Honestly, it sounds more like *content*, and it suits you."

Mallory smiled. "Thanks, I'll take it."

Her phone buzzed on the table. She walked over and picked it up. She found a text from Jonah.

You home? No one answered the door. Got something 4 U.

She couldn't prevent the smile that slid across her lips. She looked up to find Mom watching her.

"That must have been a message from Jonah."

"What makes you think that?"

"Your smile. It's a look saved for someone special. You may not think it now, but I think he's your someone special."

Mallory shook her head and rolled her eyes. "Mom."

"You're not disagreeing."

Mallory glanced at her watch. "Thanks for lunch and helping with the festival, but I need to head back to the farm."

"Sure thing, honey. I'm glad we could have this time together." Mom stood and opened her arms.

Mallory walked into her embrace and breathed in the soothing scents of home—vanilla and sunshine.

Ten minutes later, she shifted her oversize purse on her shoulder and turned onto the driveway to the farm. Because of the warm weather and the closeness of the ranch, Mallory had enjoyed the walk to and from lunch with Mom.

As she passed the dirt road that led to the cabin, she glanced up the hill and found Jonah's truck parked in front.

She paused.

Should she head to the cabin or go to the farmhouse?

Trying not to overthink it, she headed up the hill.

Country music spilled out through the screen door as she stepped onto the very neat front porch. Two Adirondack chairs sat on either side of a small round table to the left of the door, overlooking the hill. To the right of the door, a large potted plant sat on a metal stool.

She tapped the back of her hand against the door frame, but no one answered. Cupping her eyes, she peered through the screen. "Jonah?"

She couldn't see too well into the small space, but what she could see showed spotless living quarters. His rack had been made and the blankets tight under the mattress. The tabletop was clear. No dishes sat in the sink. The room smelled faintly of lemon oil.

So much better than the pine oil used on the ship when she'd been on sea duty. That scent was permanently burned into her brain.

He'd turned "rustic" into an enjoyable living space.

"Mallory."

She jumped and spun around at the sound of her name.

Jonah stood behind her, cleaning his dirt-covered hands with a rag. "What are you doing here?"

"Looking for you. I was at the ranch when you texted. Instead of going to the farmhouse, I decided to see if you were here. I wanted to see how you were doing. You know, since seeing your dad."

"I'm fine." His words tumbled out in a rush. He jerked his head toward the strawberry patch. "I started weeding the rows. Berries are coming in nicely. We should have plenty for pickers by the time the festival rolls around."

Okay, discussing his parents was off-limits. Good to know.

"Great. Glad to hear it." She glanced down at her jeans and fitted pink T-shirt. "I'll change and give you a hand with the weeding."

He smiled. "I won't say no to that. I left you something on your porch. I didn't want to walk in when you weren't home."

She stepped off the porch and headed for the hill. "Walk down with me."

He shrugged and shoved the rag in his back pocket. "Sure. Sounds good."

As they headed down the hill, she shared her

conversation with her mom about the food and activities for the festival.

"Sounds like you have a great start. What can I do to help?"

Two things she'd noticed about Jonah—he was quick to compliment and quick to lend a hand. She remembered her mother's words about imperfect families and how her parents committed to making their marriage and family a success.

Mallory needed to be more like Jonah and put her feelings aside and do more to make theirs work.

At the foot of the hill, Mallory stopped next to the hoop barn and put her hand on her hips. "We need to figure out parking. Would you mind handling the logistics of that?"

"Not at all. Consider it done."

Mallory marked that off her mental checklist.

They approached the farmhouse, and Mallory spied a large box tied with pink ribbon by the door. She frowned. "What's that?"

Jonah hung back and waved her toward the steps. "Why don't you look and find out?"

She hurried up the stairs and dropped her purse on the swing. From inside the house, Hope began to bark.

Mallory reached for the box and turned it to see the picture on the front. She looked at Jonah with wide eyes. "A dog crate? You bought me a dog crate?"

He climbed the steps and sat on the edge of the swing, leaning forward and balancing his forearms on his knees. Even in grubby jeans, a sweat-stained T-shirt, and dirt on his face, he could still stop traffic. His backward ball cap caused her pulse to pick up speed. "Certainly not a romantic gift, by any means, but I thought we could use it for when Lucy is ready to come home."

Mallory wrapped her arms around the wide box and rested her cheek on top. "I love it. Thank you. And thank you for being so supportive."

He pushed to his feet and looked at her with dark eyes. "I'll do anything for you, Mal. Someday you'll realize that."

With that, he half jogged down the steps and cut through the yard toward the strawberry patch.

As she watched him walk away, she kept one hand on the box and placed another against her chest.

If she wasn't careful, he was going to steal her heart.

If he hadn't already.

Guarding it was a safer choice, even if she liked having him around more and more. Because when he changed his mind and decided she wasn't worth staying for, she didn't know if she could pick up the broken pieces again.

Chapter Nine

Mallory was adult enough to admit when she was wrong. And she was wrong about Jonah. He had changed. For the better.

Laughter drifted through the open upstairs window as Mallory stood to the side and watched Jonah chase after Tanner. He picked their little boy up over his shoulder the same way her brother-in-law had done soon after Jonah had come back into their lives.

Keeping her distance was getting harder.

Did she even want to?

At one time, Jonah was the man she never wanted to see again, but now she searched for him every time she entered a room.

But was she brave enough to take the next step?

She sat on the edge of her bed and curled her fingers around the plain narrow band that she'd worn for less than a month after their unexpected elopement.

She'd never done anything as impulsive in her life. She'd learned from that mistake.

But now…

While Tanner helped Jonah with repainting the fruit stand Bri's parents used every summer, Mallory had snuck away and finished unpacking her bedroom. Somehow, she'd managed to drop her jewelry box and scatter everything across the hardwood floor.

As she retrieved the miscellaneous earrings and bracelets, a sliver of gold rolled under the nightstand.

She pried it out, and the gold band felt like a brick in her hand.

Why had she kept it?

Maybe part of her held on to hope all those years ago that Jonah would've changed his mind and return to her. To them. But that hadn't happened. And now that he was back, she still kept him at arms' length.

They were still married. Legally, at least. And she still hadn't done anything to change that.

Maybe she wasn't ready to let go.

Mallory walked to her dresser and pulled a gold chain off her jewelry rack. She threaded the ring, then fastened the necklace around her neck and tucked it under her shirt.

Needing some air, she left the room before she changed her mind and returned the ring to its hiding spot for the past eight years.

She headed down the stairs. Her phone rang.

She pulled it out of her jeans pocket and found Bri's name on the screen. She accepted the call.

"Hey, friend. How are you doing?"

"Still trying to get unpacked, but otherwise, we're doing well. Cam's falling into a routine at the office and loves working with his dad." Bri stifled a yawn on the other end of the line.

"That's great, but how are you doing?" Mallory slid her feet into the ankle boots she wore in the fields. "You sound sleepy."

"I'm okay. I picked up a bug or something, so I haven't been feeling that great. So tired. Believe it or not, I miss the farm. I miss sitting on the porch with my morning coffee and reading my Bible. We found a nice house with a fenced-in yard for Leo to explore. Cam keeps reminding me to give Durango a chance."

Mallory pushed through the screen door and stepped onto the porch. Rosie and Hope followed and jumped onto the swing. Mallory sat in the middle and pushed her toe against the porch floor to move them. "It's so beautiful here."

"You sound… I don't know…contented, maybe. You good?"

"Yes, I am." And for the first time in quite a while, Mallory actually believed it. "I love it here. Tanner is acclimating well." Hope climbed into Mallory's lap as she told Bri about Hope's rescue and adopting Lucy.

"I hear a lot of 'we.' I take it things between you and Jonah are getting better?"

She remembered the kiss from the other day. The same one she'd been reliving since their walk with Lucy. "They're...improving. I do believe he's changed. He's quick to help with anything I need. He dotes on Tanner. And he's patient with me as I get the hang of the farm. I'm not ready to pick up where we left off, but I don't want to run in the other direction when he shows up at the house either."

Bri laughed, which made Mallory miss her friend even more. "Cam said you're planning to revive my grandparents' berry festival."

"Yes, when Jonah and I brainstormed ideas about the farm, I thought of the festivals they used to do and suggested it. He was all for it. He's been taking such great care of the berries. I've updated the website and social media accounts with daily progress reports, hoping to raise interest for when we kick off the season. We've gained more followers, so that's a plus."

"See, I knew you two would work it out."

Mallory held up a hand, then realized her friend couldn't see her through the phone. She dropped it in her lap. "I wouldn't go that far. We have a long way to go. Both of us. But we're taking things one day at a time."

Jonah and Tanner raced across the grass and headed for the porch. Jonah fell back and let Tanner charge ahead. He smacked the railing, then thrust his hand in the air. "I win! Mom, I beat Dad."

Mallory glanced at Jonah, and he winked, which sent a jolt through her stomach. Jonah jogged over to Tanner and ruffled his hair, then they sat side by side on the top step. Tanner leaned his shoulder against his dad's.

If Mallory hadn't been on the phone, she would've snapped a picture of the tender moment.

"Hey, Bri. Jonah and Tanner are here, so I need to go. I'll give you a call later if you're going to be around."

"Sure, that sounds great. And, Mal?"

"Yeah?"

"It's great to hear you sound so happy."

Mallory laughed as she ended the call, but her friend's words lingered. She slid her phone into the front pocket of her hoodie and set Hope on the swing next to Rosie. She stood and moved behind her guys.

Wait a minute.

Her guys?

Jonah turned and looked up at her, his sunglasses shielding his eyes, but his smile could stop her heart.

Tanner swiveled in his spot. "Hey, Mom, guess what?"

Mallory crouched behind him and ran a hand over his hair. "Tell me."

"Did you know Dad used to ride bulls like Uncle Bear?"

She smiled as a memory returned of teenage Jonah competing in a rodeo arena along with her brother.

"I did know that. I believe he won a few buckles too."

Tanner's eyes widened as he looked at his father with hero worship. "You did?"

Jonah nodded but didn't elaborate. Did his mouth just tighten?

"Can I see them?"

"Well, I don't have them. I think they're still at Grandpa's place."

That explained the lack of enthusiasm.

Tanner jumped down the three steps and waved his dad to follow him. "Come on. Let's go get them."

Jonah chuckled. "Hold up, bud. Your mom and I have things to do. The festival's coming up, remember?"

Tanner kicked at the grass with the toe of his worn sneaker. "Aw, man."

"Tell you what—grab some lunch while I finish up a few things at the cabin, then I'll swing by Grandpa's place and see if I can find them." Jonah's jaw tightened again.

Mallory had a feeling his dad's was the last place he wanted to be since learning his mom was back in the picture, but she also had a feeling he'd suck it up, because he'd do anything for his son.

She reached for the screen door. "Come on, Tanner. Get washed up for lunch, then we'll go into town with your dad." She glanced at Jonah. "If you don't mind."

His shoulders relaxed and his mouth softened into a smile. "Not at all."

Mallory jerked her head toward the house. "Want something to eat?"

Jonah shook his head. "Thanks, but I do need to finish up a few things at the cabin. I'll text you when I'm done and see if you're ready to go."

Mallory nodded, then headed into the house. While Tanner washed his hands, she made a couple of PB&J sandwiches, set one on a plate along with carrot sticks and apple slices.

Tanner ran into the kitchen and hurled himself into the chair by the window. He took a bite of his sandwich, glanced at her with a guilty look, and then folded his hands and recited a quick prayer.

While Mallory ate her sandwich, she made another one for Jonah, but instead of peanut butter and jelly, she added turkey and swiss between two slices of his favorite rye bread.

Less than ten minutes later, Tanner downed the last of his milk and wiped a hand across his mouth. "I'm done. Can we go find Dad?"

Mallory pulled out her phone and waved it. "He said he'd text."

"Yeah, but he was just being nice. We can go to him."

Mallory tidied the kitchen, then followed Tanner outside, holding the screen door open. As he shot across the yard, she patted her hand against her leg. "Come on, girls. Let's go find Jonah."

Rosie launched after Tanner while Hope hesitated on the porch. Mallory scooped her up and followed her son. As she rounded the hoop barn and headed up the hill, she lost sight of Tanner, but for once she wasn't worried. He was safe on the farm, and that was helping her sleep better at night. Plus, with Jonah close by, she was beginning to feel more secure than she had in a long time.

As the cabin came into view, Mallory followed the sound of a saw whining as it tore through wood. Tanner crouched in the grass and pointed. "Look, Mom, a frog."

She held up a hand. "Keep it there. We have enough pets."

Frogs weren't high on her list of cuddly animals.

Mallory continued to the side of the cabin and found Jonah, with his shirtless back to her, feeding a board through a table saw. Wood chips flew around him, but her eyes were riveted to the faded scars lining his spine.

Rosie barked and danced around his feet while

Hope pawed at Mallory's shoulder. She pressed a hand against the trembling dog's small back.

Jonah stopped cutting and switched the saw off. He petted Rosie. "Hey, girl. What are you doing up here?"

Then he turned and saw Mallory standing near the corner of the cabin. "Oh, Mal. Hey. Sorry. I didn't hear you." He reached for a gray T-shirt that had been tossed behind him and pulled it over his head.

She turned away, but she'd never be able to erase the physical evidence of what he'd endured. She lifted a hand in a pathetic wave. "Tanner didn't want to wait for your text, but I see you're still busy. Stop down when you're ready to head into town." She turned and headed for the narrow dirt road.

"You don't have to go."

His words stopped her.

Oh, yes she did.

She turned around. He grinned and took a step toward her.

Her heart rate spiked.

"I'm just cutting wood for the elevated beds. Now that you're here, you can give me a hand."

"What about me, Dad? Can I help?" Tanner ran up to him.

Jonah wrapped a gentle arm around Tanner's neck. "Of course, buddy."

While Rosie and Hope sat in the sunshine,

Mallory helped Tanner hold one end of the board while Jonah attached the sides to the legs with a nail gun.

A warm breeze frisked Mallory's face as the thwapping sounds of the nail gun mingled with Tanner's chatter. And Jonah didn't get annoyed with his millions of questions even once. He explained every step with details Tanner would understand and even allowed him to help.

Even though Mallory had a thousand things of her own to do for the festival, she didn't want to leave.

Growing up, she'd seen how her dad had spent quality time with her brothers and longed to have that same paternal mentoring for her own little boy.

And now he had it.

Even though Jonah never mentioned taking off again—in fact, he insisted he was there to stay—Mallory still couldn't shake the feeling it was only temporary. She kept waiting to wake up and find Jonah gone because he decided they weren't worth sticking around for.

But what if she was wrong this time? What if he did stay? What would that mean for them in the long-term?

She wanted more than co-parenting, but that meant letting go of her fears and trusting Jonah with her heart once again.

She wasn't quite ready.

She just hoped he'd continue to remain patient until she was.

Heading to his dad's house was the last thing Jonah wanted to do. But he'd given his word to Tanner, and he'd keep it.

He'd dropped Mallory and Jonah at the diner, where they planned to chat with her aunt and uncle about food for the strawberry festival.

Good thing, because he didn't want Tanner caught up in his family's drama.

As he turned into Dad's driveway, he was relieved to find it empty. He pulled up to the closed garage, and no lights appeared to be on inside the house.

Maybe he could get in and get out and his dad wouldn't even know he'd been there. Jonah wasn't in the mood for a confrontation.

With his engine still idling, Jonah gripped the steering wheel as he tried to make sense of what he had seen the other day.

Why would his mother come back to town and not tell him?

Why keep it a secret?

Especially if she and his dad had been seeing each other for a few months already. It just didn't make sense.

A shadow fell over the dash, and someone knocked on the driver's-side window, startling

Jonah. He jerked his head around and found his dad standing by the truck.

Jonah lowered the window.

Dad rested an arm on the door frame. "So, how long are you going to sit here before you find the courage to head inside?"

"Courage? That would imply that I'm afraid."

Dad raised an eyebrow. "Well, aren't you?"

Jonah scowled. "What do I have to be afraid of?"

His dad shrugged. "Don't know. But you ran out of here the other day like your tail was on fire."

Jonah unbuckled his seat belt and opened the door. Pocketing his keys, he got out, slammed the door and then glared at his dad. "I didn't run. I walked out. Mom's the runner, remember?"

Dad held up a hand. "No matter how you feel about her, she is still your mother. And you will show her some respect."

"One thing the marine corps taught me is that respect is earned."

Dad dropped his gaze and just shook his head. Then he lifted a hand and rested it on Jonah's shoulder. "Son, I know you're upset. Let's head inside and talk this out."

"What's to say? You kept this from me. Mom's been back in town for who knows how long, and she didn't try to contact me. What's up with that?"

"She was afraid."

"Of what?"

"Of how you'd react. And if I may say so, her fears were a little justified."

"Dad, what did you expect? I find you and Mom kissing in the middle of the living room like it was no big deal. It's a big stinking deal. She left us. She left you, and she left me."

"That's in the past. Your mother has changed. She's back now. For good."

Jonah rolled his eyes. "Whatever."

"You don't think she's changed?"

Jonah shrugged. "How should I know? I haven't heard from her once in the past twenty years. No phone calls for my birthdays or Christmas. Nothing but silence. I find her in your house, and I'm supposed to open my arms and welcome her with joy?"

"Isn't that what you expected Mallory to do?"

Jonah narrowed his eyes. "That's a low blow, and you know it. My situation with Mallory is different."

Dad moved behind Jonah, placed his hands on his shoulders and turned him to face the side mirror on the truck. "Look in the mirror. Who do you see?"

"Dad, I don't have time for this. I just stopped by to grab something out of my old room for Tanner. He and Mallory are waiting for me at the diner. I really don't want to hash out our family history."

"Who do you see?"

"Seriously? I just said I don't have time for this."

Dad's hands tightened on Jonah's shoulders. "Who. Do. You. See?"

Jonah ground his jaw and looked in the mirror. Instead of seeing the man before him, with more lines on his face and gray in his hair, Jonah remembered a younger version of his father sitting on the edge of his favorite chair, sobbing as he held a crumpled piece of paper in his hand.

Jonah swallowed. Hard. His eyes burned as he stared at his own reflection, a younger version of his father. But as he looked closer, his father's blue eyes looked clear. The lines in his forehead had smoothed out.

"I see the kind of man I want to be." He shook off his father's hands and turned. He lowered his voice, the fight gone from his words. "I want to be like you, Dad. I've always admired you. You were so strong and brave after Mom left. You dealt with all the junk I put you through. After I'd gotten in trouble with a couple of kids from the rodeo circuit, Uncle Stu gave me a choice—juvie or the military. I chose the marine corps because I wanted to make you proud. When I got hurt, I was too ashamed to come home. I know you would've welcomed me home with open arms.

You forgive quickly—me, and it looks like you've forgiven Mom. I want that. I do. There's just so much…hurt and resentment and anger. I need to work through that before I can forgive her. Before I can even talk to her."

Feeling drained, Jonah leaned against the truck door.

Dad dragged a hand over his face and shook his head. "You're wrong, Jonah. I wasn't strong and brave after your mother left. Held it together for your sake. But just barely. She broke me. I'm not gonna lie—I hated her for what she had done to me, but mostly to you. You were growing up without a mother. What you don't know, what I kept from you, is your mother struggled with depression. Before she'd left, we found out she was pregnant, but she lost the baby shortly afterward. It messed with her head, and she struggled to cope. I suggested she see a counselor or someone who could help her see through the grief she was experiencing, but she put me off. Said she didn't want to burden some stranger with her problems. She left a note saying she needed some time to find herself. I will say she regrets her actions deeply. More than anything, she wants you to forgive her so she can be the kind of mother you deserve."

Jonah waved a hand toward the house. "Where is she? Why are you telling me this and not her?"

"She's back at her place in Texas. She's packing up her apartment so she can move back home."

"Home? This hasn't been her home in twenty years."

"I never stopped loving your mother and held on to hope that she'd come back someday."

"Then you were a fool."

"Why? Why is me holding on to hope any different than what you're holding on to with Mallory?"

"Mallory didn't leave me."

"No, Jonah. You left her. So try to remember how you felt when your mother walked out on you. Don't put yourself in Mallory's shoes, because they just won't fit. Instead, walk alongside her and let her know that you understand what she's feeling. Then give her the time and space she needs to heal from that pain. As for your mother, she loves you very much. And she wants nothing more than to be a part of your life. But that choice is yours." His dad waved a hand toward the house. "You're welcome to come in. This place will always be your home. But whenever your mother is here, you will treat her with respect, whether you think she deserves it or not."

Without another word, Dad walked toward the mailbox, leaving Jonah standing in the driveway alone with his thoughts and the afternoon sun beating down on his head.

Jonah gripped the back of his neck, then shoved his other hand in his pocket. "Dad."

Heading toward the house, his father turned, the mail in his hands. "Yeah?"

"How'd you do it?"

"Do what?"

"Forgive her."

Dad took another step toward him. "Wasn't easy. When she first called, I hung up on her. Then she called again and asked if we could talk. I told her no and to stop calling me. But your mother has a mind of her alone. Instead of calling a third time, she showed up. I'd just gotten home from the university and found her waiting in the driveway. I invited her inside. The moment she stepped back through the door she'd closed twenty years ago, she started to cry. I felt like a jerk, so I let her talk. After she left, I called my pastor. He put me in touch with a counselor. For years, I kept my feelings bottled up and needed a safe place to let them out. I met with my counselor twice a week for a few months. And I prayed. I asked the Lord to soften my heart. Then I realized I'd never have peace until I forgive Gayle. So I did, but that forgiveness was more for me than it was for her."

Jonah caught the shimmer in his father's eyes, and his own throat thickened. He took a step toward him. "I'm glad you were able to do that for yourself. I know how anger can eat you up."

"Forgiveness is a process, son. It doesn't happen overnight. Your mother and I cannot go back to the way we were. That relationship is over. We were different people. Now we're older and wiser and can make better choices moving forward. You're past the age where I can tell you what to do. I can only hope you will make the choice that's best for you and your family. Pray about it and ask the Lord to lead you." Dad squeezed Jonah's shoulder, then headed inside the house.

Jonah stood in the driveway with his hands in his pockets, his father's words echoing inside his head. He'd wanted Mallory to forgive him and pick up where they left off. But that was for his own selfish purposes. No wonder she kept him at arm's length.

He opened the truck door and slid behind the wheel. As he backed out of the driveway and headed toward the diner, he realized he'd forgotten to get the belt buckles. While he didn't want to let Tanner down, he needed some time to think. And pray. So he could be more like the man his father was.

If he could forgive his mother for walking out on him, then maybe, just maybe, Mallory could forgive him for doing the same to her.

Chapter Ten

Mallory's to-do list was longer than her arm. She needed more hours in the day to get everything accomplished before the upcoming strawberry festival.

And that meant she didn't have time to think about Jonah. And the fact that she hadn't seen him since yesterday after he had visited his dad. When they returned from town, he dropped her and Tanner off at the farmhouse and headed to the cabin, claiming he had work to do.

He hadn't even come back to tuck Tanner in for the night, which had been a first since they'd moved onto the property.

Darkening clouds lumbered across the sky, squeezing out the morning sun. The cool air drifted across the valley, and Mallory shivered in her T-shirt. She should've grabbed her hoodie.

With the sunshine warming her back, she treaded lightly between the rows of fruit. Berries as long as her thumb ripened in varying shades of pink to nearly crimson.

Tanner ran one of his toy dump trucks through a pile of dirt Jonah had removed from the berry beds.

She shielded her eyes and looked over at Jonah, who had been weeding the long rows since first thing this morning. "You've done a great job. The beds look amazing."

"Thanks." He shot her another one of his devastating grins. Then he pushed to his feet and arched his back, his face twisting.

"You okay?"

"Nothing a couple of pain relievers won't help."

"The other day..." Mallory paused.

"Yeah?"

"I saw your back. You know, when you were cutting the framing for the elevated beds. I'm really sorry for what you've gone through. I wish I had known."

"Known? Why? I was a complete jerk to you."

Mallory lifted her shoulder. "I can't imagine going through something like that alone."

Jonah laughed, but there was no humor in his tone. "Alone? I was surrounded by people. All kinds of doctors and nurses and therapists. I was never alone."

"That's not what I meant." She rubbed the dirt off her fingers.

Jonah walked with his arms stretched out for balance until he reached her. He grabbed her hands and gave them a gentle squeeze. "I know.

I appreciate it. Some of the toughest years of my life."

"Mind telling me what happened?"

"The day I received your signed papers in the mail, my unit was sent out on patrol. I was distracted and second-guessing myself for even filing. Our convoy hit an IED. I was thrown from the vehicle and landed against a crumbling rock wall, breaking my back."

Mallory sucked in a breath as her hand flew to her mouth. "Jonah…"

"I spent over a year in and out of hospitals, undergoing numerous surgeries to repair the damage to my spine. I went from doing missions to not being able to walk. Once the swelling and inflammation finally started to go down, then my nerves stopped screaming, and I could regain some feeling in my legs. It took several surgeries to repair my back. I'll never be one hundred percent, but I am grateful for every day I can take a step. I never want to be in a wheelchair again."

"I won't pretend to know what that was like, so I'll save the empty platitudes."

"I appreciate that. After being medically discharged and forced out of career I'd come to love, I hit bottom. I drowned my sorrows and guilt in pain pills and alcohol. Then I met Micah Holland, who understood what I was going through. His family started a program to give veterans a second chance. He's the reason I'm who I am today."

Mallory stepped closer and pressed a hand to his chest. "Don't cut yourself short. You had to do the hard work."

"Speaking of hard work..." He took her hands. "Mal, I've been thinking. About us."

"What about us?"

"Yesterday I had it out with my dad in the driveway at his house."

"About your mom?"

"Yeah. And he said something that hit a nerve. I guess I needed to hear it."

"What's that?"

"I walked back into your life and I expected to pick up where we left off. But we can never do that. And I realized I don't want what we used to have."

"You don't?"

Shaking his head, Jonah pulled off a glove. He lifted a hand to her face and caressed her cheek with the pad of his thumb. "No. Because I'm not that guy anymore. And you're not the same girl I married. We've both changed. I am so very sorry for the way I hurt you, for the way I sent you those papers like a coward. I've been asking you to forgive me as if that will fix everything. I realized I wanted your forgiveness to take away my own guilt. That's my problem to work through, not yours. I hope you can forgive me someday, but for yourself."

Jonah's face blurred in front of her, and she

reached up and covered his hand. "I have to be honest, Jonah. When you walked into the farmhouse with Cam, my first instinct was to grab Tanner and flee the state." She paused as that memory returned. "I wanted nothing to do with you. I didn't want to give you any more opportunities to hurt me. But it wasn't just about me. I wanted to protect Tanner as well. He is my world. Learning to share him with you has been a challenge, but, you've stepped up. You're the kind of dad he needs. Even though you are still the same kind and generous man I married in Virginia, I also see how you've changed to become the man you are today. I guess I was a little afraid to forgive you."

"Why's that?"

"My unforgiveness became a fortress. An insulator against future hurts. If I forgive you, then that would make me vulnerable. I don't want to be hurt again."

Jonah slid a hand around Mallory's neck and closed the distance between them. "I'll never hurt you intentionally again."

Before she had time to think, time to weigh out the pros and cons, time to talk herself out of doing it, Mallory leaned forward and brushed her lips across his.

He pulled her close as he kissed her.

With trembling fingers, Mallory slid her finger along the chain hanging around her neck and lifted it from beneath her T-shirt.

His eyes widened as he spied her wedding ring on the chain. "Is that…?"

She nodded. "I found it the other day. I'm not ready for it to go on my finger, but right now it's around my neck as a reminder of the promises we made all those years ago. When I recited them, I meant them at the time, including for better or worse. I do forgive you, Jonah. I'm still asking for time and patience."

"Babe, I will give you whatever you want. I would like to have a serious conversation about what the future holds for us as a family."

"I know, and I appreciate that. Can we put that on hold until after the festival and a decision is made about the farm?"

A smile spread across Jonah's lips. "Absolutely. You've given me hope. And that's enough for now."

A large raindrop splattered on her nose. Mallory lifted her face to the sky and found the clouds overhead had turned almost smoky. She whistled. "Rosie. Come on, Hope, let's head inside. Let's go, Tanner, before we get soaked."

Before she could take another step, the sky opened, pelting them with cold rain that made her catch her breath.

She squealed and tried to shield her face. Jonah hooked an arm around Tanner and tossed him over his shoulder like when they'd been playing. Then he grabbed Mallory's hand. Together, they raced across the wet yard, trying not to slide in the slick grass. Both dogs charged ahead of them.

They dashed onto the porch as a roll of thunder echoed across the valley, sounding like someone shaking a giant sheet of metal. Slashes of lightning lit up the fields and cast everything in an eerie gray-yellow glow. Minuscule balls of ice assaulted the ground, bouncing off everything they hit.

"I don't like the looks of that sky. Hail is never a good sign." Jonah dropped her hand, then raked his fingers through his soaking-wet hair. He lifted the hem of his T-shirt and wiped his face. "You okay?"

"Yes, but we need to dry off." Mallory opened the door.

Tanner scooted under her arm, then held open the door. "You coming, Dad?"

Jonah glanced down at his jeans and shirt, which dripped tiny puddles around his feet. "Sorry, bud. I'm already drenched. I'm just going to make a run for it and head back to the cabin."

"Are you sure? You're welcome to wait out the storm inside."

"I don't want to get everything wet. I'll be fine." Without another word, he dashed down the steps and raced across the grass, ducking from tree to tree.

With Hope cradled against her chest, Mallory crouched in the doorway so she could see and waited for a light to come on inside the cabin. Once she was sure he was safely inside, she headed into the farmhouse and closed the door against the storm raging across the valley.

"Tanner, go upstairs and change into dry clothes. Please put your wet ones in the hamper."

She carried Hope into the kitchen, then retrieved some old towels out of the laundry room. "Let's get you girls dried off."

She rubbed their wet fur, then wrapped them in dry towels and set them on their beds in front of the electric fireplace. She flicked the switch. Within seconds, a flame licked the faux logs and generated heat in the chilly room.

She headed upstairs to change out of her own clothes and to check on Tanner. She peeked into his room. "You okay, Tanner?"

He'd changed into a red T-shirt and a clean pair of jeans. But his wet clothes remained in a soggy pile on the floor.

She pointed to his clothes. "Hey, you know where those go. Pick them up and put them in your hamper."

"Aw, Mom." But he did as he was told. "Where's Dad?"

"He went back to the cabin."

Tanner's shoulders slumped. "Man, I wish he lived here."

Part of her wanted to agree with him, but she remained quiet and headed to her room. She changed into yoga pants and a dry hoodie that still smelled like her favorite fabric softener. She dried her hair and twisted it into a messy bun.

Nobody to impress but her son and the dogs, and they didn't care.

She peeked back into her son's room and found him connecting small blocks on his bed. "Hey, buddy. Want something to eat?"

He rolled off his bed. "I guess."

Mallory gave his shoulder a squeeze as they headed for the stairs. As they reached the bottom step, thunder rumbled and rolled as lightning crackled, illuminating the room in an electric glow.

A snap and loud pop sounded outside. Everything went dark, including the fireplace. Tanner jumped and wrapped his arms around her waist, clinging to her side. "Mom, what was that?"

Mallory reached for his hand and guided him down the steps. "It's the storm. Lightning must've hit a transformer."

"What are we gonna do? How can we watch TV?"

"We can read or play a game."

"What about Dad?"

"I'm sure he's fine."

Someone pounded on the door. Mallory pulled it open. Jonah was wearing a hooded raincoat, but he shrugged out of it and left it outside. Then he stepped inside as another crack echoed.

"I just wanted to check and see if you guys were okay. I lost power at the cabin."

"We're without electricity, too, but we're fine otherwise."

Jonah reached into his back pocket, pulled out a flashlight. "This was all I had at the cabin."

Mallory headed for the kitchen. "I'm sure we have candles in here somewhere. This is not the first storm Aspen Ridge has seen."

Crossing in front of the sink, she glanced out the window. Then stopped. She closed her eyes and opened them again. Her heart sank.

She gripped the edge of the counter. "Jonah."

"Yeah? You find them?"

Nibbling at her bottom lip, she shook her head and pointed out the window. "Look."

He stood beside her, his shoulder touching hers. Then he released a sigh. "The beds."

Hail covered the strawberry beds as if snow had fallen.

"What are the odds the berries are safe?"

Jonah looked down at the sink and shook his head. "I don't know. We can't assess anything until the storm ends. Right now, it's not safe to be out there. And there's nothing we can do anyway."

Mallory's pulse picked up speed as her heart hammered against her ribs. She tried to swallow, but her mouth was dry. "We need those beds to be okay. Without them, we won't have much of a strawberry festival. Without that festival, we won't be able to turn a profit on the farm. And without that, then we won't be able to buy it. We'll be letting down Bri and Cam."

Jonah turned to Mallory and cupped her face in his hands. "Mallory, breathe."

He pulled in a deep breath, his chest rising. She did the same. As he released his air, she released hers. Then he slid his arms around her and pulled her to his chest. "We will make this work. I promise. You're not in this alone. We'll face it together."

Together. She rested her cheek against his chest and listened to the steady beating of his heart.

Yes, they were in this together. For better. For worse. And whatever else may come.

Jonah needed to come up with a plan because he wasn't going back on his word to Mallory. She needed—no, *they* needed—the festival to be a success so they could move forward with buying the farm and restoring their family.

Problem was, he didn't know how to fix it.

The storm dumped more rain than the strawberry beds could absorb. Even though the sun was out, puddles lay in the rows, covering berries that had nearly been ready to be picked. Hail had broken some of the fragile vines, damaging some of the crop.

Jonah dragged a hand over his face, his eyes burning from lack of sleep. The morning sun scalded the back of his neck as he skirted the ruts between the rows of berries and squished through the mud.

The lower beds were submerged, while the upper beds seemed to be saturated but not under water. Maybe there was hope.

Maybe.

Pounding echoed across the field, and Jonah felt every strike of the hammer like a blow to his temples.

He made his way to the edge of the patch and trudged across the open field, where Bear and Wyatt reworked the old Wallen fruit stand that suffered some damage in last night's storm.

As he neared them, he lifted a hand. "Hey, guys. Thanks for your help."

"When family calls, we come." Bear spoke around a nail jutting from the corner of his mouth. "You look like you were dragged through the storm."

"Thanks, man. Always appreciate a good compliment."

Bear lifted a shoulder. "Just sayin'. What's going on?"

"Lack of sleep. Spent half the night trying to keep Tanner calm and Mallory from stressing."

"You spent the night at the farmhouse?" Wyatt's eyes narrowed.

His tone got under Jonah's skin. "Dude, we are married, you know. But no. Once the storm stopped, I carried Tanner to bed and headed back to my place." He jerked a thumb over his shoulder toward the cabin.

"Sorry, I guess I forgot about that."

"No worries." Jonah nodded toward the stand. "Need a hand?"

"Nah, we got it."

"Thanks again. I'm going to check on Mallory and see what I can do to help her."

Halfway to the farmhouse, his phone vibrated in his front pocket. He pulled it out and found his cousin's name on the screen. "Hey, man. How's it going?"

"Dude, I heard about the storm. Wanted to check and make sure you're all right."

Jonah dragged a hand over his weary face. "We're...fine."

"That doesn't sound promising."

"No, man. It's all good. The three of us are safe. The beds, well, they took a beating from the hail and rain."

"How bad?"

"Not sure yet. The upper beds will be fine, I think. Parts of the lower beds are still underwater. I'm hoping we can salvage some of them. The festival's next weekend."

"Yeah, Bri and I plan to head down for it."

"Staying the weekend?"

"Nah, just a day trip. To be honest, I'd be a happy man if I didn't have to stay more than a few hours on the farm again. That life's not cut out for me."

"So does that mean you and Bri want to sell?"

"Yeah, I think so. And that's part of why I wanted to call. We found a house that Bri loves, so we submitted an offer—waiting to hear back on that. Dad invited us to attend his church. While we miss our friends and family in Aspen Ridge, I can see us settling in Durango."

"That's great, man. I'm happy to hear all's going well for you."

"Yeah. So you think you and Mal may be buying the farm?"

"I hope so. We hope the festival's a success and plan to talk once that's over."

"Lloyd Burton is getting antsy and called again with a higher offer."

"Of Burton Industries? That's who wants to buy the farm?"

"Yes."

"What did you tell him?"

"The money he offered was pretty sweet, but I said it wasn't an option right now."

Cam named a figure that constricted Jonah's breathing. "I can't pay close to what he's offering."

"Hey, bro, I'm not asking for that. From you or Mal. We'll stay with the appraised price. Bri and I want you guys to have it. I just wanted to touch base and see if that was still a possibility."

"You sure you want to unload this place? It's so peaceful here."

"I'll admit, it's a great piece of land, but I don't have the time it deserves. I wanted to make Bri happy when we got married, but I'm not cut out to be a farmer."

"I never expected to be one, either, but the longer I'm here, the less I want to leave."

"And that's all about the land? Nothing to do with the cute brunette staying at the farmhouse?"

Jonah laughed. "Oh, she has everything to do with it. But the property is nice too. I really want this to work, Cam. If she can learn to trust me, then maybe we have a shot at a future again."

"You talk about needing Mal's trust. Maybe you need to trust the Lord and His will—for your life. And the farm, even if the outcome isn't what you're hoping for. Listen, I gotta run. Like I said—I wanted to touch base and see where things stood with you two and the farm."

"We still have a little time left before our deadline, so don't be swayed by the commercial buyer's dollar signs yet. I'm still hoping to win Mallory's heart by then."

"I'm rooting for you guys." With that, Cam ended the call.

Jonah curled his fingers around the phone. His cousin was right—he'd been so focused on regaining Mallory's trust that he'd kind of forgotten to do trusting of his own. What if the outcome wasn't what he'd been hoping for? Could he live with that?

Jonah couldn't win over Mallory on his own, but with the Lord on his side, at least he had a fighting chance.

Chapter Eleven

Mallory shouldn't have doubted Jonah. And not just about the festival. When he promised to make sure they'd be able to pull everything together, he followed through with his word.

Their hard work was paying off.

After the storm had nearly destroyed their crop, Mallory was ready to give up. But not Jonah. He was a fighter. With the scars to prove it.

So why had she spent so much time doubting him?

For the last week, he'd been up at the crack of dawn and hit the rack long after the stars came out. Once the beds dried out, they salvaged what berries they could. Jonah started replanting so they could have a crop a little later in the summer.

She'd helped him place the seedlings from the greenhouse in the elevated beds. After putting Tanner to bed, they spent evenings designing brochures highlighting the benefits of buying into Jonah's CSA project.

She finalized the food her aunt and uncle would be selling.

Finally, the day of the festival arrived. Cars lined the empty field they'd designated for parking, and visitors wandered through the maze of activities her family had helped coordinate.

Upbeat music from a playlist Everly had compiled streamed through an external speaker near the barn and competed with the conversations and laughter filtering through the air.

Everly stood near the gate and passed out flyers detailing the day's events and directed visitors where they needed to be.

Dad and Cole manned the small petting zoo while Wyatt offered roping lessons. Bear's Lil Riders Rodeo group showed off their skills and invited other kids to join them.

Callie painted strawberries on faces while Piper oversaw the vendors' booths displaying work from local crafters and artists.

Macey helped three little girls create handprint strawberries with red and green paint.

Mom stood at a table next to the fruit stand and demonstrated how to make strawberry freezer jam to a group of teenagers from their church.

As Mallory passed her table, Mom handed her a bright red strawberry. Mallory bit into it and savored the sweetness.

Aunt Lynetta and Uncle Pete closed the diner for the day and directed their customers to the farm, where they manned their new food truck, which offered Uncle Pete's famous barbecue pork sandwiches along with strawberry short-cake, strawberry milkshakes and strawberry pie that made Mallory's mouth water.

She needed to find her family so they could grab something to eat.

With the cloudless blue sky, warm sunshine and a gentle breeze, the day was practically per-fect, and she wasn't about to allow anything to ruin it.

Mallory simply couldn't have done any of it without Jonah and her family.

As she passed the lower beds, pickers hunched over rows in various shades of green as they filled their quart baskets with berries. Every now and then someone let out a whoop and held up a large, ripe fruit.

With her stomach grumbling even louder, Mal-lory shielded her eyes and scanned the property, searching for Tanner.

She found him standing next to Jonah, his small hand tucked inside his father's large one. They stood in front of one of the newly-con-structed adaptive beds, talking with a man wear-ing tan cargo shorts and leaning on crutches.

She paused and snapped a photo—one of dozens she'd taken already. She skirted around her nieces, Lexi and Avery, chasing each other through the apple orchard.

As she approached the bed, her heart slammed against her rib cage. Hours spent in the sunshine had bronzed Jonah's skin. His broad chest filled out the red T-shirt he wore.

Tanner grinned at her and waved. "Hi, Mom."

She reached them and gave him a quick side hug. "Hi, honey. Having fun?"

Tanner nodded so hard his hat, which matched Jonah's, nearly slid back off his head. She righted it and smiled. "I'm glad."

He jerked a thumb at Jonah, who shot her a wink that sent her pulse racing. "We're telling Mr. Rose about the 'portance of adabive...wait..." He turned to Jonah. "What did you call it again, Dad?"

"Adaptive." Jonah enunciated the word clearly.

"Yeah, that." Tanner turned back to Mallory. "Adaptive farming."

At that moment, the man who had been talking with Jonah turned. Mallory let out a gasp. "Patrick? Patrick Rose? Is that really you?"

The blond-haired man smiled widely. He settled his crutches under one arm, then held out a hand to her. "Mallory Stone, as I live and breathe. I thought you were off seeing the world."

"I could say the same for you. My time in the navy was up last year, so I returned to Aspen Ridge."

"That's fantastic. And you look great, by the way. Civilian life seems to suit you." Then he darted a look between Tanner and Mallory. "Wait a minute—did the little guy just call you 'Mom'?"

She nodded and wrapped an arm around Tanner's shoulders. "Yes, Tanner is my son."

Patrick jerked a thumb toward Jonah. "And he's Tanner's father?"

Mallory looked at Jonah. He regarded her with a raised eyebrow and an amused smile on his face. Before she had time to change her mind, she moved between Tanner and Jonah and reached for his hand.

His warm calloused fingers curled around hers and gave her a light squeeze. "Yes, Jonah is my… my hus—" Her mouth dried as her throat tightened. She turned and coughed into her shoulder. "Excuse me. Apparently, I need some water."

Jonah released her hand and picked up a bottle sitting by his feet. He uncapped it and handed it to her. She smiled her thanks, then drank half, her fingers tight around the container. She cleared her throat. "Sorry about that. Jonah is my husband. We've been married eight years."

This time, the word didn't stick in her throat. In fact, just saying it seemed to release some of the pressure building in her chest.

Jonah squeezed her fingers as he ran his thumb over the back of her hand.

"Wow, that's great, Mallory. I'm happy for you."

"Thanks." She turned to Jonah. "Patrick's parents have the Rusted Rose Ranch on the other side of Aspen Ridge."

Was it her imagination, or did the lines soften around Jonah's mouth? Did he consider the younger guy a threat?

For as much as she'd always liked Patrick, he wasn't her type.

Jonah, on the other hand...

No, don't go there.

Mallory nodded toward the crutches. "What happened?"

Patrick rolled his eyes and shook his head. "Slipped while trying to hook a bonefish in Belize. Jimmied up my knee and needed surgery, which ruined the rest of the season for me."

"Ouch! I'm sorry to hear that." She turned back to Jonah. "Patrick is a world-class fisherman with an online streaming channel."

"That's pretty cool, man."

"Thanks. I was living the dream until I made that rookie mistake. Getting antsy to get back on the water." Patrick nodded toward one of the elevated beds. "Your husband was just telling me about his idea for adaptive gardening. Now that's cool."

Mallory's chest swelled as she looked up at her husband. "Jonah wants everyone to have the same opportunities. If the elevated beds are a success, then he'll be partnering with the local veterans association and offering their members the opportunity to grow their own produce next year. They'll learn skills and have a stake in the outcome."

Jonah slid an arm around Mallory's shoulders. More than anything, she wanted to lean into his embrace and stay there for the rest of the day.

Or maybe even the rest of her life.

"We want to offer more opportunities to those with disabilities and limited mobility who enjoy gardening to be able to continue that activity."

"What you guys are doing is great." Patrick pulled his phone out of the front pocket of his cargo shorts and snapped a picture of the two of them. "Not bragging or anything, but my streaming channel has nearly two hundred thousand subscribers. I'd love to do a live chat from the farm and give you a little exposure."

"You call two hundred thousand a little?" Mallory's eyes widened. "Are you serious?"

"Sure, anything to spread the word. I do a feature on Fridays, highlighting positive role models I see in my travels. Why not shine a spotlight on the hometown girl and her hubby doing good work?"

"Thanks, I appreciate it—*we* appreciate it. And Jonah's local too. He and Bear used to do the rodeo circuit together."

Patrick frowned a moment, and he held out a hand as his jaw dropped. "Wait a minute—you're Jonah Hayes? *The* Jonah Hayes? I used to love watching you ride broncs when I was a kid."

Jonah lifted a shoulder. "That was back when I was a punk and thought I knew everything—but thanks, man."

"Why'd you stop riding?"

Jonah glanced at Tanner. "Got into some trouble and was offered a choice—enlist or do some time. So I joined the marine corps."

"Man, this keeps getting better and better. No wonder you have a heart for veterans. You are one. Thank you for your service." Smiling, Patrick stuck out his hand. "Both of you. You're doing a great thing here. Keep it up." His phone chimed, and he dug it back out. He looked at the screen, then back at them. "Listen, I gotta jet. My buddy's in town for the weekend, and I want to see him before he and his family head back to Denver. Great meeting you, Jonah." He pulled Mallory into a quick side hug. "Good seeing you again, Mal."

"You, too, Patrick. Thanks for stopping by."

"I'll be in touch."

Jonah stood behind Mallory and slipped his arms around her waist. "That's the first time you called me your husband. I could get used to hearing it."

She could get used to saying it.

Maybe she was ready to trust him and move forward to strengthen their relationship.

One day at a time.

Jonah knew better than to get cocky. But hearing Mallory introduce him as her husband caused him to walk a little straighter, and with a bit more strut in his step. Plus, it didn't hurt that she hadn't left his side since joining him while he was talking to Patrick Rose.

When Jonah tried to take her hand, though, she'd pulled away.

Baby steps.

At least things were moving in the right direction.

If Mallory hadn't shown up when she did, would they've been given the opportunity to be part of her friend's fishing channel? Even though their lifestyles were completely different, Jonah was still appreciative of any opportunity to share his and Mallory's visions for the farm. And if it could help more people, then so be it.

With the sun beating down on them, they passed the fruit stand where people paid for the berries they'd just picked or purchased ones he and Mallory's brothers selected from the fields yesterday.

Kids with red-stained lips carried half-eaten

strawberry snow cones, courtesy of Pete and Lynetta.

Tanner yanked on Jonah's arm. "Dad, can I get a snow cone?"

"Sure, buddy. Let's head to the food truck." They wove through the growing crowds.

A reporter from the Aspen Ridge Times stopped Mallory. "Mallory Stone? Mind answering a few questions about the festival?"

She smiled at the woman. "Not at all." Then she glanced at Jonah. "You guys go ahead. I'll catch up."

Jonah hesitated. Should he be a part of the interview too?

Tanner jerked on Jonah's arm. "Daaad."

"Okay, I'm coming." They made their way to Pete and Lynetta's food truck and waited behind several people.

The savory scent of Pete's barbecued pork made Jonah's mouth water. Once they reached the window, Tanner ordered a snow cone, which Jonah insisted on paying for. He'd wait to eat with Mallory, who was walking toward him.

She reached him and grabbed his arm. "I set up an interview for later so she could talk with both of us. Hope you don't mind?"

"Mind? Not at all? Hungry?"

"Famished."

Before they could order, someone called his name. "Jonah!"

He turned and found Cam and Bri hurrying toward them.

They stepped out of line, and Jonah slung an arm over his cousin's shoulders. "Hey, man. When did you guys get in?"

"Just now."

"I love your shirts." Bri wagged a finger between Jonah and Mallory, then opened her arms and gave them a group hug.

"Thanks." Mallory pulled back and glanced down at her pink shirt. "I designed a new Wallen Fruit Farm logo with red shirts for our guy helpers and pink ones for the girls."

Bri turned in a slow circle, then faced Mallory and gripped her forearms. "You two have done an amazing job. This takes me back to the festivals my grandparents used to put on. They'd be so proud, Mal."

Even though Mallory wore sunglasses, from his angle, Jonah could see her rapid blinking as she appreciated her friend's words. "Thanks, Bri. That's what I was going for—a similar feel as the ones from our childhood." Then she turned to him. "Jonah's been amazing. I thought we were done after that terrible storm, but he's worked his tail off this week to get everything ready. We barely saw him."

Cam clapped Jonah on the back. "Welcome to the world of farming, my man. Hope you enjoyed your previous vacation because it will be your last."

Jonah laughed. "Well, my last vacation was our honeymoon, so I guess I can't complain."

As expected, Mallory's cheeks turned a bright pink, and she turned away from him slightly.

Cam lowered his mouth closer to Jonah's ear. "Glad to see you two are getting along a little better."

Feeling like Tanner when he got excited, Jonah could barely stop himself from bouncing on the balls of his feet. Barely. "Earlier she introduced me as her husband, so that's progress. And she's been wearing her wedding ring on a chain around her neck, so I think we're moving in the right direction. I'm trying not to rush her."

"Good plan, man. The last thing you want is to drive her away. Speaking of good news, I wanted to let you know—"

Someone called Mallory's name.

She laid a hand on Jonah's arm and looked at Cam and Bri. "Excuse me. I'll be right back."

He watched her head toward the food truck.

"There's my son."

His mother's excited voice sent a chill down his spine. Next to him, Cam stiffened.

She reached for Jonah first and planted a kiss on his cheek. More than anything, he wanted to rub away the evidence of her affection, but that would be petty, and he wasn't thirteen.

"Hi, Mom." He reached around her and extended a hand to his father. "Dad."

"Hey, Jonah." Dad took his hand and clapped a hand on his upper arm, squeezing lightly. When he'd been a kid, that had been his dad's signal to behave. He met his father's eyes and gave him a slight nod. Message received.

"Hey, Aunt Gayle." Cam kept his arms pinned at his sides, even as Jonah's mother released him from one of her octopus hugs. Then he nodded to Jonah's dad. "Uncle Leland."

Dad extended a hand. "Cam, good to see you."

"You, too, sir." Cam shook it quickly, then dropped it and moved behind Jonah. "If you'll excuse me, we need to grab something to eat." He headed for Bri and pulled her toward Lynetta and Pete's food truck.

Mom's eyes followed them, her lips turned down. "My nephew doesn't want anything to do with me either."

"Can you blame him?" The words escaped before Jonah had time to catch them.

He sighed and gripped the back of his neck. "Sorry for the tone, but I can't apologize for the words. You walked out on all of us, Mom. You can't expect to pick up where you left off, no matter how much you want to."

Mom dropped her chin to her chest and nodded, then she looked at him with what appeared to be genuine tears in her eyes. "I know. I just..."

Her voice trailed off as she lifted her shoulders, then dropped her hands at her sides. "I know I don't deserve you after what I've done. I just want a chance to explain and apologize. Will you give me that?"

His father's words about change, forgiveness and second chances echoed through his head. Laughter drew his attention to the food truck, where Cam and Bri talked with Mallory's parents.

Deacon and Nora Stone had been the epitome of a devoted couple—something he'd always wished his parents had been. No wonder he seemed to have spent more time at Stone River than at his own house after his mom had left.

Deacon pulled Nora close and pressed a kiss to her temple. She looked at him with adoration in her eyes—the same look Mallory had given him earlier. A look he hoped to see more and more.

"Listen, Mom. I can't talk right now." He waved an arm over the crowd. "We're pretty busy with the festival. How about if we get together tomorrow?"

She nodded, the light in her eyes still dim. "Yes, okay. I'll have to be satisfied with that, I suppose. I'm sorry to barge in like this, anyway. We'll leave so you can enjoy the rest of your day."

His mother's aim-to-please attitude set his teeth on edge. "It's a public event, open to the community. Everyone is welcome. Enjoy the food. Pick some berries. Get your face painted. Just don't make a scene. Please."

Her lips thinned, deepening the lines around her mouth. "I don't plan to make a scene." Then she grabbed his father's arm. "Come on, Leland. Let's go."

Dad scowled at Jonah over the top of his mother's head, his disappointment quite clear. Jonah wasn't a kid anymore, and he wasn't about to placate his parents in exchange for his own peace of mind.

He let out a sigh.

Mallory hurried across the grass and touched his back. "You okay?"

He nearly nodded, then shook his head. He needed to be honest with her, even with the hard stuff. "I just… I don't know. I don't even want to see her. I mean, after she left, I prayed and begged God to bring her back. Now that He's finally answering a ten-year-old's prayer, I don't want her in my life."

"Why not?"

"Because I'm afraid of the pain if she decides to leave again."

"I get that."

Those three words, spoken quietly and without malice, felt like a prize fighter's fist to the gut.

Jonah turned slowly and reached for Mallory's arms. He searched her eyes, hidden behind her sunglasses. "You do understand. Because of me. I'm so sorry, Mal."

"Hey." She pressed a hand against his jaw. "That's not what I meant. I wasn't trying to shift the blame. But, to be honest, I understand your fear because I've felt it every single day since I saw you walk through Bri's front door. If I get too close and you break my heart again, I don't know if it could be repaired a second time."

He took her hands and enveloped them with his. "What if I promise not to leave? Promise not to break it?"

"One day at a time, remember?"

He nodded. "Right. Let's grab a bite to eat."

"Hold on." She pressed a hand against his chest. "I just wanted to say thanks and let you know how proud I am of you. I can see how hard you've been working, and it's paid off. The festival is amazing. Even if we don't break even, I still consider today a huge success."

"Thank you." He could barely get those two words out with the thickening in his throat. He didn't deserve her, but he'd cherish her words.

He needed to put his mother out of his mind and enjoy the rest of the day with Mallory by his side. He truly hoped today was a turning point in their relationship.

Chapter Twelve

Mallory was a little afraid to get her hopes up, but the increasing number on the calculator had her grinning.

Was it possible?

Had they actually turned a profit from the festival?

She hit the equal sign, then squeezed her eyes shut.

She opened her right eye and peered tentatively at the screen. Realizing the number wasn't a mistake, she thrust both fists in the air and let out a whoop at the top of her lungs.

Rosie and Hope raced over to her, barking at the noise that had interrupted their afternoon nap.

The front door slammed open. "Mallory!"

Heavy footsteps thundered across the floor.

Mallory hurried into the living room. "Jonah, what's wrong?"

Seeing her, he stopped short and shot her a scowl. "You tell me."

Now it was her turn to be confused. "What are you talking about?"

"I just heard you yell. I thought you'd gotten hurt, so I came running."

Mallory clamped a hand over her mouth, but that couldn't contain the burble of laughter climbing up her throat. She threw her arms around his neck. "I'm fine. In fact, I'm more than fine. We did it!"

"That's great." Jonah slid his hands around her waist. "What did we do?"

She laughed. "We turned a profit with the festival! In spite of the damage to some of the lower beds, we were still able to have enough berries to sell. Plus, the sign-ups for the CSA generated even more money. We did it. Wait, I take that back—*you* did it."

His eyes softened. "No, you had it right the first time. We're a team, remember? We did this."

"I was ready to quit at the first storm, but you remained steadfast, determined to turn something beautiful out of the damage that had been done by the hail."

"You weren't ready to quit. You just needed to find your hope and hold on to it." Jonah lifted Mallory off her feet and spun her around gently. "Thank you, Lord."

He set her back down so her feet touched the floor, but he didn't release her. As he drew her close, she breathed in the scents of sunshine and hard work, along with the subtle scent of fabric softener from the threads of his T-shirt.

At that moment, she didn't want to be in any other place than in her husband's arms.

Her husband.

The title rolled around inside her head as Jonah gazed at her. The way his blue eyes darkened and seemed to roam over her face, she struggled to put any coherent thoughts together.

Her hands slid to his shoulders, then she trailed her fingers through his hair. She swallowed as her eyes pulled away from his.

She shifted on her bare feet and took a step closer, bridging the gap between them.

Before she had time to think, time to weigh out the consequences, she tugged him down gently to her and brushed a kiss across his lips.

Jonah pulled her against his chest. With one arm still wrapped around her waist, he trailed a finger along the curve of her cheekbone and jaw. "You are so beautiful."

She rested her cheek against his chest, listening to the rush behind his rib cage.

She hadn't been the only one affected.

"We need to talk."

Any other time, those four words would've filled her with dread. But now, in this moment, she considered the impact they would have on their future.

A future she could picture with the two of them together, being the family their son deserved.

Her watch vibrated on her wrist. She glanced at the time and realized it was her alert to pick up Tanner. She placed a hand on his chest. "I agree, and I want to talk. I do. But I want it to be when we have some time without being rushed. I have to pick up Tanner from school shortly. How about staying for dinner tonight? I'll cook something to celebrate."

He enveloped her hands inside his. "Let's do it together. We can throw some steaks on the grill and eat outside."

"That sounds like a great idea. I need to clean up this mess quickly before I leave." She glanced at the papers spread across the kitchen table and left the security of his arms. Reluctantly. She stacked the receipts neatly, clipped them together and tossed them in the basket.

"Mal?" Jonah reached for her arm.

She dropped her calculator into the basket next to the receipts. "Yeah?"

"When was the last time you took time for yourself?"

"What do you mean?"

He laughed, the rich timbre of his voice skating over her. "The fact that you responded with that question answers mine."

She shook her head. "No, I guess I meant to ask why you wanted to know."

He took her hands again. "Why don't you let me pick up Tanner while you stay here and relax. Take a nap. Go for a walk. Read a book. Do something just for you."

"But…" She was quick to voice dissent, but why?

Why didn't she want Jonah to pick up their son? What was she afraid of?

Releasing control? Relying on someone else?

As she took in his questioning eyes that still radiated peace, she considered the past couple of months where he'd done nothing but bend over backward to prove himself. And he'd done just that—proven he was a trustworthy father to Tanner and a trustworthy man to her.

Slowly, she turned her fingers until they intertwined with his and she gave them a gentle squeeze. "Okay."

"Okay?" His eyes widened. "You serious?"

"Yes, I am. The idea of reading more than a page in my book sounds glorious." She snatched her keys out of the bowl on the counter and handed them to him. "Take my car and pick up Tanner. His booster seat's already in the back. But promise me one thing."

"Anything. You name it."

"Tanner gets distracted and likes to wander. Promise me you won't take your eyes off him."

He held up three fingers, and his pinkie touched his thumb. "Scout's Honor."

She grabbed his hand and pressed a quick kiss against his lips. "I'd believe you if I didn't already know you'd gotten kicked out of Cub Scouts for putting that frog in Mrs. Nelson's backpack."

His smile widened, deepening the lines at the corners of his eyes. "I still stand by my innocence. Bear put that frog in her backpack. I was framed. But I didn't get kicked out. I had to choose between Cub Scouts and Vic's Lil Riders Rodeo. Like any good country boy, I chose horses and rope tricks over merit badges and olive shorts."

She lifted her hands. "Hey, I just know what Bear said."

"And your brother never stretched the truth?" His grin tripped her pulse. Then his eyes grew serious. "Mal, you can trust me. I promise to keep my eyes on Tanner at all times. I won't let you down." He pulled his keys out of his front pocket and handed them to her.

As his words showered over her, for the first time since that conversation in the same kitchen where she'd learned they were still married, Mallory believed him.

He was the kind of husband she'd always wanted, and he'd been so patient waiting for her to receive his words.

A rush of tears filled her eyes, and she smiled. "I trust you."

Just saying those three words lifted a weight

off her. Little by little, she could hear the imaginary bricks falling away from her heart.

Their future together was just beginning, and she couldn't wait to have the conversation with him after dinner. Hopefully, he felt the same way.

Jonah held Mallory's fragile trust as if it were a delicate spiderweb. Strong for its purpose but easily destroyed. And he didn't want to go down that road again.

Now that Tanner was safely secured in the back seat of Mallory's car, it was time to head home.

Home.

One of his favorite four-letter words.

Hopefully, after tonight, their home would look different than it had in the past couple of months.

As they pulled out of the pick-up lane, Jonah caught sight of the blooming bush in front of the school. He glanced in the rearview mirror. "Hey, buddy. How about we stop and pick up flowers for Mom?"

Grinning, Tanner nodded. "Can we go to Miss Marigold's? I visit her with Nana sometimes."

"Sure." Jonah headed toward Main Street and parked in front of the shop across the street from the diner. He cut the engine, then opened Tanner's door. He grabbed his son's hand as they stepped onto the sidewalk. "Remember to stay with me and don't wander off."

"Okay, Dad."

The yellow storefront stood out among the neutral tones of the other businesses. Potted plants and flowers in various colors and sizes sat in clusters around a faded blue vintage bike under the large display window.

They climbed the three steps lined with more colorful pots and opened the door. Bells jangled against the glass.

Jonah pocketed his sunglasses and gave his eyes a moment to adjust to the lighting. The wooden floor creaked as they moved past the coolers to the displays of arrangements in a multitude of sizes and colors.

"There's so many." Tanner's eyes widened as he turned in a circle in the middle of the shop. "How will we be able to pick?"

"Afternoon, fellas. How can I help you?"

Jonah turned and smiled at the woman wearing a white T-shirt, jeans and a yellow apron with *Marigold's* in black script. Her short, gray hair had been styled away from her face. Long, dangling earrings bounced every time she moved her head. Folded glasses hung from a chain around her neck.

Tanner pulled free from Jonah and rushed over to the woman, wrapping his arms around her waist. "Hi, Miss Mari."

She returned the hug, then crouched to meet

him at eye level. "Hello, Tanner. How's my favorite seven-year-old doing today?"

"Good." He beamed at her, then turned to Jonah. "This is my dad."

Jonah shortened the distance in two long strides and held out his hand. "Nice to see you, ma'am. Jonah Hayes."

She took his hand and covered it with her own. "Jonah Hayes, of course. Leland's boy. I remember you when you were no more than Tanner's size."

Of course. Miss Mari had been a staple in Aspen Ridge and the church where his father attended. Having been away for so long, Jonah had forgotten. But he had a sudden image of her standing in their doorway with a covered plate.

"You brought us cookies. My dad and me. After my mom…" His words trailed off as he glanced at Tanner.

"That's right. We'd had a Sunday school picnic the weekend prior, and you said you loved my oatmeal butterscotch cookies the best, so I brought you a batch."

"You have no idea what that meant to me. And I haven't had a cookie yet that could live up to yours."

She gave his hand a gentle squeeze as her smile caused her eyes to crinkle in the corners. "You're so kind. How can I help you this afternoon?"

"I'd like to get some flowers for my…wife."

Still saying the word didn't feel real, but what he felt for Mallory wasn't imaginary.

Miss Mari glanced at Tanner, then back at Jonah. "You're married to Mallory Stone, aren't you?"

He nodded, not wanting to say more.

"I saw the two of you at the strawberry festival. Beautiful couple."

"I'm sorry I missed seeing you. There were a lot of people."

She waved away his words. "You only had eyes for the young lady at your side." Taking his elbow, she turned him toward the display shelves. "Would you like something premade? If nothing here suits you, I can create a bouquet in a few minutes. What's your wife's favorite flower?"

Jonah pressed his lips together as he scanned his brain. Had he bought Mallory flowers when they were together? Did she mention having a favorite?

"Mom likes tulips. She said they need strong roots for the winter so they can grow and bloom in the spring. She said they give hope." Tanner looked at him and grinned.

Jonah ruffled the boy's hair. "Thanks, buddy. That's perfect."

Miss Mari walked to the cooler and pulled out a tall container of colorful tulips. "Tulips mean deep love. They also symbolize rebirth. And Tanner's right—they do offer hope."

"I'll take a dozen in different colors."

"Dad, I'm thirsty. Can we get a drink at the diner?" Tanner pointed a finger toward the front window. "It's right there across the street."

Jonah glanced at him. "Yes, in just a minute. Okay?"

Tanner heaved a sigh. "Okay."

Miss Mari carried the container of tulips to a counter behind the register. As she arranged them in a vase, Jonah turned and scanned the rows of arrangements.

He needed to buy flowers for Mallory more often.

The front-door bells hit the glass as another customer walked in. Jonah glanced over his shoulder but didn't recognize the dark-haired woman who entered. He returned his focus to the arrangements as the lady talked with Miss Mari.

"Jonah, your flowers are ready. There are cards on the counter if you want to include a message." Miss Mari pointed to a narrow rack filled with cards then turned to the counter behind the register.

Jonah moved to the register and scanned the display of cards. He chose one with pink hearts, picked up the pen chained to the counter and thought about a message.

"Dad—"

Not turning around, Jonah held up a finger. "One more second, buddy."

The front door opened again as Jonah finished his note.

Hopefully, Mallory wouldn't find it too cheesy.

He slid it into an envelope, then reached for his wallet. "Thanks, Miss Mari. What do I owe you?"

She moved to the register, punched a few buttons and gave him a total. He counted out the bills and handed them to her.

Picking up the vase, he admired the greenery and bow she'd included. "Thanks. Mallory's going to love them."

As he pocketed his change, he turned toward the door. "Okay, Tanner. Let's head to the diner."

Not getting a response, Jonah turned, but Tanner wasn't behind him.

His heart jumped. Bracing the vase against his shoulder, he bent sideways to see if he could see his son in one of the other aisles. But he wasn't there.

Jonah cupped a hand around his mouth. "Tanner! If you're hiding, you need to come out. It's time to go."

He paused for a moment but heard nothing. He strode back to the register and placed the vase on the counter. "Miss Mari, have you seen Tanner?"

Her brows pulled together. "No, hon. He was with you."

"*Was.* I'm going to leave these tulips here and see if he's outside."

"I'll put them in the cooler until you return." She picked up the vase and carried it across the room.

Jonah wrenched open the door and jumped the three steps to the sidewalk, which sent a jolt of pain up his back. Shielding his eyes against the rays of sun that nearly blinded him, he scanned both directions of the walk.

No sign of his son.

Sweat slicked his face as his blood turned to ice. He closed his eyes and let out a slow breath, forcing his adrenaline to calm.

Lord, I could use some help here.

His phone rang in his front pocket. He fished it out and found Mallory's name on the screen. He gripped the phone and ground his jaw.

Of all the people who could call... Talk about imperfect timing.

Jonah swallowed. Hard. Raking a hand through his hair, he accepted the call. "Hey, Mal."

"Hey, you. Just wanted to check and see how long you're going to be so I know when to start the grill."

As he surveyed the sidewalk once again, he wavered about his response. Telling her he'd lost their son would destroy that fragile trust between them. But not telling her would do the same thing when she found out the truth.

A band tightened around his chest. "About that... I don't know."

"What's wrong?"

"I can't find Tanner."

She paused a moment, each second ticking away at the alliance between them. "What do you mean you can't find Tanner?"

He told her that he'd run a short errand and when he went to pay, Tanner was gone.

"Stay where you are. I'm heading into town." She ended the call before he had time to respond.

The one time she trusted him with their son and he'd messed up. Big time.

Chapter Thirteen

Mallory's nightmare about something happening to her son was becoming a reality. She never should've trusted Jonah to pick up Tanner from school.

Now her son was missing.

She found her car parked in front of Miss Mari's flower shop and pulled Jonah's truck in behind it. She gripped his keys and jumped out, slamming the door behind her.

With her heart in her throat and the adrenaline thrumming through her veins, she shoved her sunglasses on top of her head and stood on the sidewalk in front of the flower shop and searched in both directions.

Jonah was nowhere to be found.

Great. Now they were both missing.

She hurried up the steps to the flower shop and pushed through the door.

Miss Mari rounded the corner of the register. "Did you find him?"

"Him?" Mallory frowned. "You mean Tanner?"

She nodded.

How'd she know their son was missing?

Mallory shook her head. "No, I saw my car parked in front of your store and wanted to pop in and see if you'd seen Jonah."

"He was here a few minutes ago. I wanted to help him find Tanner, but my assistant is out making a delivery, so I couldn't leave the shop."

Mallory reached for Miss Mari's hand and gave it a gentle squeeze. "No worries. We'll find him."

Her words sounded hollow to her own ears.

Tossing a goodbye over her shoulder, she stepped outside and closed the door behind her.

"Mallory!"

She turned at the sound of Jonah's voice. He jogged up to her, red-faced and hair damp with sweat.

"Did you find him?"

Jonah shook his head, his lips pressed. "Not yet."

"That's why I said not to let him out of your sight. He tends to wander." Mallory ground her jaw.

"I know what you said. And I didn't. He was with me the entire time."

Mallory lifted her hands and dropped them to her sides. "Apparently not, because he's not with you now. The one time you have him and you lose him."

Jonah dropped his gaze to his feet and shook his head. "I screwed up. Let's just find Tanner."

She swiveled on her heel. "I'll check the diner. Maybe Aunt Lynetta saw him."

Jonah smacked his hand against his forehead. "The diner! Of course."

"What about it?"

"He mentioned being thirsty and wanting to go to the diner. I told him to hold on until I took care of business."

Her eyes narrowed. "What kind of business?"

"We'll worry about that later. Let's go check the diner." He grabbed her hand.

They hurried down the sidewalk and stopped at the crosswalk. Just as the light turned red and the symbol flashed for them to walk, the diner door opened. Aunt Lynetta stepped out, holding on to Tanner's hand.

"Tanner!" Glancing quickly both ways, Mallory dashed across the street. She dropped to her knees in front of her son and wrapped her arms around him. "Baby, I'm so glad you're safe."

He wriggled out of her arms. "Of course I'm safe. Why wouldn't I be?"

Jonah's shadow stretched over them as he reached for Tanner. "Buddy, I'm so glad you're safe."

"Why does everybody keep saying that?"

Jonah scowled as he took Tanner by the shoulders. "How did you get to the diner?"

Tanner's eyes widened at his dad's tone. He scrunched his face and pointed to the sidewalk. "I... I walked. How else would I get here?"

Jonah blew out breath. "Why did you leave me?"

"I asked if I could go to the diner. You said one more seccond. The second was up, so I went."

Jonah dragged a shaky hand over his face as he pushed to his feet. "I meant, in just a second I would go with you. I needed you to be safe."

Tanner's chin wobbled as he rubbed his eye. "Aunt Lynetta took good care of me like she always does."

Mallory reached for her aunt. "Thank you so much."

"Of course, sugar. What's going on?"

"Tanner didn't tell his dad that he was leaving wherever they were. Jonah's been searching for him. I called to see when they would be coming back home and learned my son was missing."

"*Our* son." Jonah spoke from behind her.

Mallory stiffened. "Right. Our son."

"I'm glad everything worked out." Aunt Lynetta cupped Tanner's chin. "You, young man, stay with your parents next time." She pressed a kiss to his forehead.

Tanner's bottom lip puffed out as he kicked the sidewalk with the toe of his sneaker. "Yes, ma'am."

Mallory wrapped an arm around his shoulders,

then dug Jonah's keys out of her pocket. She held them out to him. "May I have my keys please? I'll be taking Tanner home."

He gave her a look. "Don't you think you're overreacting just a little?"

She didn't know whether she should laugh or scream.

"Overreacting? You're seriously asking me that? You lost our son."

"I get that you're upset, and I'm sorry." He slapped her keys in her hand. "This wasn't something I set out to do."

Heat crawled up her neck. She glanced at her aunt and Tanner, who watched their exchange. She gave him a curt nod. "Let's discuss this at home."

With her hand still on Tanner's shoulder, they headed for the crosswalk. Jonah's words echoed with every step.

Even if he didn't mean to lose their son, how could she trust him to keep Tanner safe without her being present?

The elation she'd felt earlier disappeared, along with her confidence in Jonah. She had no idea where to go from here.

For the first time since moving to the farm, Jonah dreaded going to the farmhouse. But he needed to talk to Mallory, and Tanner, about what had happened earlier. Putting it off wouldn't help anyone.

He knocked on the screen door and waited. He expected to hear the sound of Tanner's running feet, but silence fell over him.

He pushed the door open and stepped inside. "Hello?"

The muted sound of a conversation came from the kitchen, so he headed in that direction. Stopping in the doorway, he found Mallory sitting at the table, her back to him and her head in her right hand while she held the phone with her left. "So, once I sign the paperwork, then we're good?"

She paused and nodded. "Okay, great. I'm looking forward to having it done and finalized."

Finalized? What paperwork was she referring to?

She ended the call, then folded her arms on the table and rested her forehead on them.

He coughed quietly.

She jumped, then swiveled in her chair and glared at him. "Jonah, what are you doing sneaking up on me?"

"I knocked, but you didn't hear me. I came to check on Tanner." He peered over his shoulder at the living room blanketed in silence. "Where is he?"

"He's not here. He's at the ranch." She pushed

to her feet and faced him, her arms folded over her chest. "What do you want?"

He lifted his hands and dropped them. "I just told you—I came to check on Tanner."

"And I just said he's not here."

He was not in the mood. "Fine."

Then he jerked his chin toward the phone on the table. "Talking to your divorce lawyer?"

Her brows pulled together. "What are you talking about?"

"I heard you say you're looking forward to having it done and finalized."

She made a face. "Very funny. I was referring to Lucy's adoption. She is recovering well from her surgery. Irene said she'll be ready to leave the shelter this week."

"Sorry. Bad joke." A ridiculous amount of relief swept over him. So much so that he sagged against the door frame. "That's so good to hear."

"I just don't know if it's the right choice, especially now." She turned away from him and faced the window that overlooked the side yard.

He moved behind her. "Why do you say that?"

Mallory remained quiet.

"Mal, what's going on?" He touched her arms and felt her stiffen, so he dropped his hands at his sides.

She turned slowly and looked up at him, blinking rapidly. Her eyes shimmered. "We need to talk."

Earlier, those four words had filled him with hope. Now they tightened his gut. He ran a hand over his face. "Yeah, we do. We need to discuss how to handle Tanner's disobedience."

"I can't talk about Tanner right now." She waved a finger between the two of them. "We need to discuss us."

"What about us?"

"Losing Tanner is my greatest fear."

"It's any parent's greatest fear. I get that, Mal. I do. I was terrified when I turned around and he wasn't there." He paused and rubbed a fist against his sternum where the ache hadn't gone away. "If something had happened to him, I wouldn't be able to live with myself. He was by my side the entire time."

"Not the entire time. Otherwise, you would've seen him leave. I told you he likes to wander and you promised to watch him."

Her words spoken softly and threaded with pain lanced his chest. The delicate trust she'd gifted him had been destroyed by one moment of carelessness.

It was more than carelessness. He lost their kid.

There was no way to sugarcoat it, No apologies would make it better or change what had happened.

His stomach a tangle of knots, he crouched in front her and took her hand. "I failed you. I failed Tanner."

Again.

The invisible word hung in the air between.

"I am so sorry. I'm not an irresponsible person. Something like this will never happen again. Give me another chance. Please."

He wanted to take her in his arms and do whatever it took to take away her fears. But, that would push her further away from him.

"I love you, Mallory. I loved you when I put that ring on your finger, but I love you even more today. You're an amazing mom, a tenderhearted animal lover and you give so much of yourself to take such good care of others. You deserve to have someone to take care of you. And I want that person to be me."

He'd wanted his profession of love to be romantic with the gorgeous bouquet of tulips he'd forgotten at Miss Mari's, candlelight and maybe even some soft music so they could dance in the living room after Tanner went to bed.

He'd hoped it would be the beginning of something permanent.

A tear slipped over her lower lashes and drifted down her cheek. She didn't move to brush it away. She lowered her head, breaking eye contact with him.

He touched her chin and lifted it so he could see her beautiful face. "Do you want that too?"

She swallowed, and several more tears slid down her face. She pulled his hand away but didn't release it. "I've seen how much you've done since we've moved to the farm. I've seen the way you've shown up time and time again for Tanner. I've seen how you've helped me."

"But…"

She shook her head and let go of his hand. "But I don't know if I can trust you."

"Even after all I've done to prove I've changed, it's not enough to erase what happened today."

"You screwed up, Jonah."

Those four words hammered his skull. He pushed to his feet and turned away from her as the same fear from earlier raced through him.

"I will relive that terrifying moment over and over."

She wrapped her arms around her waist. "What am I supposed to do with that?"

He sighed and scrubbed a hand over his face. "Nothing. I realize there's nothing I can do or say to change the fact that I messed up. I let you down. There's no excuse."

How could he convince her to trust him again when he doubted his own abilities to be the kind of father Tanner deserved?

Were they better off without him?

"So what you are saying?"

"I don't know. But if you can't trust me, then what are we doing? If you want out of this partnership," he paused and wagged a finger between them. "With the farm and our marriage, then tell me now so I can find some way to help my cousin, because I'm not going to bail when things get tough. Not this time."

She stared at him with wide eyes as his words lingered in the air.

When she remained quiet, he sighed. Deeply. "No matter what happens between us, I want to remain a part of Tanner's life, even if it means supervised visits again." Unexpected tears flooded his eyes as the words got caught in his throat. He backed up toward the door. "Let me know what you'd like to do."

With that, he pivoted and strode toward the front door. He closed it quietly behind him. As he moved to the steps, a pain shot through his lower back, and he nearly dropped to his knees. He gripped the railing and staggered down the steps. Though his muscles ached, he could take meds to relieve the pain. There was no cure, though, for his broken heart.

Chapter Fourteen

Of all the stupid choices Mallory had made in her life, allowing Jonah to walk out the door felt like the worst.

And she'd done nothing but watch him go.

What was her problem?

The look of anguish on Jonah's face as he closed the door behind him would be imprinted forever in her memory.

She wrapped her arms over her chest and gripped her elbows. Maybe by adding enough compression, she could keep her heart from smashing into pieces.

Doubtful.

The damage had been done. By her.

As her stomach twisted and a chill pebbled her skin, she stood at the window, staring through the glass.

She needed to go after him.

And say what?

That she loved him?

Did she love him? Love him the way he deserved? If she did love him, wouldn't she be able to trust him without condition? Without fear or worry or any of the other emotions that bullied their way into her brain?

Blowing out a breath, she headed for the door and stepped onto the porch. As she closed the door behind her, the sound of an approaching vehicle came down the hill.

Jonah's truck appeared, going faster than necessary, shooting past the barn and heading for the road. He didn't even stop. Or look in her direction. He checked for traffic and pulled onto the pavement.

Mallory stumbled to the front step and nearly collapsed on the sun-warmed wood. She buried her face in her hands and allowed the tears to flow.

A few moments later, she dragged the hem of her shirt across her eyes, then pushed to her feet. No matter how she felt, she still had to take care of Rosie and Hope.

Tires crunched on the gravel in the driveway.

Mallory ran her forefinger and thumb over her eyes and pulled her sunglasses from on top of her head and settled them on her nose. She finger-combed her hair and forced a smile in place as Miss Mari from the floral shop exited her vehicle, holding on to a vase of colored tulips.

Spying Mallory, she waved. "Hello, dear. I wanted to drop these off on my way home. Jonah forgot them at the shop in his hurry to find that dear Tanner."

Mallory hurried down the steps and met her halfway up the walk. "Miss Mari, you live in town. This was out of your way."

Miss Mari reached her and handed her the bouquet. "Oh, I don't mind the occasional delivery, especially when I know my flowers will bring joy to the recipient." She tapped the card sticking out of the back of the arrangement. "That one loves you, you know."

As Mallory took the glass vase, she could only nod.

Miss Mari turned and headed back to her beige sedan. She reached for the door, then paused and sighed. "Ah, young love. Such a beautiful thing. Don't let anything come between you two. Have a good evening, dear."

Mallory watched her back out of the driveway in a watery blur. She ran a thumb over one of the satiny petals, then reached for the card and read Jonah's scrawl.

Miss Mari says colors have meaning. White stands for hope. I'm hopeful for our future together. Yellow stands for happiness. I'm happiest when I'm with you and Tanner—my family. Red stands for true love. You are my

*true love. I hope I can spend the rest of my
life showing you just how much I love you.
Forever yours, Jonah.*

He loved her.

He'd said as much in the kitchen, but she'd been a fool quick to blame instead of listening to what he had to say.

A fresh wash of tears glazed Mallory's eyes and spilled down her cheeks. She carried the bouquet into the house and set it on the table next to her phone.

Picking it up, she scrolled through her favorites, then tapped Jonah's name. She bounced from foot to foot as the phone rang and then went to voicemail. Hearing his voice directing the caller to leave a message caused her heart to leap. "Jonah...can we talk?"

Her voice choked on the last word, and she didn't want to fall apart on his voicemail, so she ended the call. She stabbed Bri's name and waited for her friend to pick up.

"Hello?"

"Bri..." The rest of the words caught in Mallory's throat. Her fingers tightened around the phone as she gripped the back of the chair. The pressure in her chest exploded, creating a pain she'd known only one other time when she received the divorce papers in the mail.

"I'm on my way." Her friend ended the call.

The chair rocked back under the weight of her grip. She righted it, then stumbled into the living room. She collapsed onto the couch, still holding the phone, and sobbed into the throw pillow.

Rosie pawed at her and Mallory shifted. Her canine companion jumped up and nestled next to Mallory's chest, rubbing her nose against Mallory's neck and licking her chin. Hope jumped up on the other end and settled beside Mallory's hip.

Tears spent, Mallory lay in silence as the room grew darker.

Headlights arced over the wall and ceiling as a vehicle pulled into the driveway. Mallory remained where she was, not having the energy to move from her curled-up position on the couch.

Light footsteps tapped across the boards on the porch, then the front door opened.

"Mallory?" Bri called for her as she flicked on the overhead light.

Mallory squinted against the sudden brightness and pushed herself to a sitting position, rolling Hope onto the cushion. Rosie and Hope jumped into her lap.

Bri hurried over to the couch and wrapped Mallory in a hug.

The familiarity of her friend's compassionate embrace unleashed another flood of tears. Mallory sobbed against Bri's yellow T-shirt.

Rosie and Hope wriggled free and jumped down.

Bri sat on the edge of the coffee table and allowed Mallory to cry without saying a word.

A moment later, Mallory pulled away and pressed her fingers to her eyes. "I've cried more today than I have in the past six months."

"Tears are healing. At least, that's what our marriage counselor told Cam and me."

Mallory dropped her hands in her lap and accepted the tissue her friend held out. "You see a marriage counselor?"

"Mm-hmm. It was one of the conditions I made before agreeing to the trial move to Durango. Even though we'd been married only four years, Cam and I had some problems that we couldn't work out on our own. We didn't want to ignore them, so we dealt with them head-on. One of the best decisions we've made. During one of our sessions, I started to cry and apologized for my tears. Syd, our counselor, said tears are a part of the healing process. Letting them out was better than holding them in."

Mallory shredded her soggy tissue. "I don't know about that."

Bri moved to the cushion next to her. "I have a feeling you don't know about a lot of things right now."

Mallory scoffed and rolled her eyes. "You got that right. But I do know one thing."

"What's that?"

"I won't be buying the farm after all. I don't

want it without Jonah. Even though the festival was a success, I failed at keeping my family together. And my marriage..." She reached for the necklace that held her wedding band and dropped it against her chest. "That's over. For real this time."

Bri moved Mallory's hair out of the way, then unclasped the necklace.

Mallory trapped it against her skin. "What are you doing?"

Bri tugged gently and released it. She cupped her palm, then dropped Mallory's gold band into it. She set the chain on the table, then held the ring in front of Mallory. "Put it on."

Mallory frowned. "What?"

"Put it on. Put the ring on your finger."

"Why?"

"Would you just trust me and do it?"

Mallory heaved a sigh and reached for the gold band. A memory of that day on the beach, when Jonah slipped it onto her finger and promised his love for eternity, clouded her thoughts.

She ran her fingers over the gold but couldn't bring herself to put it on her finger. "I can't."

"Why not?"

"Because it's not my job."

"What do you mean?"

"Jonah put it on my finger the first time. He needs to be the one to do it again. Except now that won't happen."

"Why not?"

"Because I ruined everything. I let him go without trying to stop him."

"Did you want to stop him?"

"Yes. No." Mallory pushed to her feet and paced in front of the fireplace. "I don't know."

"What do you want, Mallory?"

Mallory turned her back to her friend and faced the fireplace, her eyes scanning Tanner's school picture sitting in the center of the mantel. "I want the pain to stop. I want a family portrait like my parents have sitting on the mantel. I want a family for Tanner so he can feel settled and secure."

Bri stood next to her. "What else?"

Mallory swallowed several times as her pulse picked up speed. The words were there. She just needed to put a voice to them. To speak them out loud. To declare what she wanted more than anything.

She looked at her friend with clarity she hadn't felt since getting the call that Tanner was missing. "I want Jonah."

Those three words released the band that had been tightening around her chest all afternoon and into the evening.

"Well, it's about time." Bri tossed her hands in the air. Then she linked her arm through Mallory's and pulled her back to the couch. "So what are you going to do about it?"

Resting her elbows on her knees, Mallory opened her hand, revealing the wedding ring she was still holding. "He loves me. Even though he told me tonight for the first time since he deployed, he's been showing me over and over. I can see that now, but I allowed our past to cloud my vision. I've been an idiot."

"No, you were heartbroken. Healing takes time, remember? It takes patience. It takes partnership. Not just with each other but also with God."

Mallory shook her head. "No, I need to figure this out on my own before I drag anyone else into my mess."

Bri looked at her with wide eyes. "I think that's seriously the dumbest thing you've ever said."

"Thanks for your support, *friend*." Mallory pushed to her feet.

"Come on, Mal. I know you're strong and independent. That's great and all, but you were not meant to go through life figuring things out on your own."

"Look around, Bri." Mallory waved a hand over the room, her voice rising. "No one's lined up at the door. Even Jonah left."

"No one's lined up at the door because you refused to ask for help. And Jonah left to cool off. Plus, he promised to help Cam with something. Had you asked, he would've stayed."

"How do you know?"

"Because I know Jonah. The man he is today. He shows up. He sticks around."

"But what if he leaves again?" Even to her own ears, Mallory's voice sounded small and tinny.

"Oh, Mal. Honey. That's what this is all about, isn't it?" Bri reached for her arm and pulled her into a hug. "You're afraid he's going to walk away again."

Mallory shook her head. "I'm afraid I won't have the strength to handle him leaving again. My family worries about me already because of these stupid nightmares. I don't want to lose Tanner or fail him as a mother."

"That's a very real fear most parents face, but that's why you need to stop trying to do everything on your own and rely on others, beginning with God. He promises never to leave us nor forsake us. Why is it you're so quick to follow authority and rules, but you won't lean into what God promises for us—promises that could lead to freedom from your fears."

"Look who's talking. Two months ago, you declared your own marriage was over."

"If I hadn't said yes about moving to Durango, it would've been. But I prayed about it, trusted God, trusted Cam, and I have to say I'm happier now than I have been in a long time."

Mallory looked at her friend, really looked at

her for the first time since she'd walked through the door. And she saw something she wanted for herself—peace.

Dropping her chin to her chest, Mallory shook her head. "I'm sorry. That was a mean thing to say."

"No apologies needed. Listen, Mal, I get it. I do. Surrendering to God will show you what true trust is all about, and that deepens your faith in Him, in yourself and in Jonah. He wants nothing more than good things for you. His plan, His purposes and His timing are perfect. Now it's up to you to decide what you truly want for your future and what you're willing to do to get it."

"When did you become so smart?"

"When I learned to say yes and get out of God's way." Bri picked up her purse. "Now, I'm heading into town and meeting Cam and his dad. Want to come?"

"Town? I thought Jonah was helping Cam."

"He is. At his dad's house."

"So he didn't go to Durango?"

"Durango? No, what made you think that? Cam and his dad are helping Leland—something about a water leak in the basement. They're moving boxes and furniture so they don't get ruined."

"And Jonah went willingly? That's going to be tough."

"He'll figure it out. Now it's your turn to figure

out a few things. Fight for what you want, especially if it includes Jonah." Bri wrapped Mallory in a quick hug. "Let me know what you decide."

Mallory grabbed her hand and squeezed. "Thanks. For everything."

"Hey, what are friends for?" With that, she headed out into the darkness, closing the door behind her and leaving Mallory alone. But this time, instead of feeling dread, hope bloomed.

Mallory walked into the kitchen, grabbed the vase of tulips and carried them into the living room. She set them in the middle of the coffee table, then picked up her laptop. Rosie jumped in her lap, and Hope curled up next to her hip.

As she stroked both dogs, she pondered Bri's parting words. Well, their whole conversation. Trust began with saying yes.

With her heart pounding so loudly she could feel it in her ears, she pushed to her feet.

She stepped outside and walked to the middle of the yard, where she had a clear view of the stars sparkling against the sky.

"Yes, Lord."

A breeze stirred through the leaves and caressed her cheeks as the sounds of the night serenaded her.

For the first time since the intruder had broken into her apartment and held her and Tanner hostage, she felt peace.

Her marriage *was* worth fighting for, and she had the perfect way to show Jonah she trusted him to stay.

No matter how loud he turned up the volume on his phone, the music through his AirPods couldn't drown out Mallory's words from earlier in the day.

You screwed up, Jonah.

Yeah, no kidding.

In more ways than one.

Why did he think the people from his past would see him any differently from whom he used to be?

Despite working his tail off, she still couldn't trust him. And that was the root of their problem.

Somehow, he needed to get Mallory out of his head. At least for the time being.

He had another problem to deal with.

His parents.

When Cam texted and asked for his help, Jonah had been quick to offer a hand, expecting to be heading to Durango. But when he called his cousin to get directions to the new house, that's when Cam said to meet him at Jonah's father's house.

Apparently, Dad had a water issue in the basement and had called his brother-in-law and nephew instead of his own son.

Now Jonah spent the last hour moving boxes

and furniture up from the basement to the garage to keep them from getting damaged.

Someone tapped him on the shoulder. Jonah dropped his box on the growing stack and twisted. Seeing his cousin, he removed one of his AirPods, which paused his music. "What?"

"No wonder you can't hear anything I've been saying. Your music is too loud."

"I like it loud."

Cam lifted his baseball hat, smoothed back his hair and placed it back on his head in a backward position. "Hope you like stocking up on hearing aid batteries too because you're going to make yourself deaf."

"Who are you? My cousin or my father?" Jonah arched his back, trying to lessen the pain shooting down his legs.

"Doesn't matter. You won't listen to either one of us."

"What's that supposed to mean?"

"You've been snarling at everyone since you set foot in the driveway."

Jonah headed out of the garage and back through the door leading into Dad's basement. "Because I don't like being lied to."

"I didn't lie to you. I said I needed your help. That was true. And you agreed."

"Yeah, but you could've led with the fact that we'd be meeting here."

"And that would've made a difference?"

Jonah lifted a shoulder.

Cam grabbed his arm. "No matter how you feel about her, she is still your mother…and my aunt."

Jonah shrugged off his hand. "Now you do sound like Dad."

"What's your problem with her, anyway?"

"Are you kidding me? How can you even ask that?"

Cam shook us head. "You don't know the whole story."

"I know enough."

"Really? Are you truly that stupid? You're living your life based on a ten-year-old's perception of what happened?"

"All I know is when I woke up that morning, she was gone. And she never returned. If I hadn't walked in on her and Dad in a lip-lock, who knows when I would've found out."

"And you've avoided her ever since."

"Not avoided—I've been busy."

"Too busy for your own mother? Listen, Jonah, I know it's tough, man. I'd give anything to have my mom back. Losing her to cancer when I was twelve wasn't fair. Wasn't right. No kid should go through what we did, but we can't change the past, right? Isn't that what you said your buddy's father kept telling you?"

Chuck Holland's words had guided Jonah when he boarded the flight in Pittsburgh for Colorado.

"Why not talk to her? Get her side of the story?"

"What's the point?"

"Dude, seriously? That's the dumbest thing I've ever heard you say." Cam folded his arms over his chest, feet spread apart, reminding Jonah of one of his drill instructors from boot camp. Shave his boy-band hair, throw him in a pair of cammies and he'd look the part. "When are you going to stop running?"

"Running? What are you talking about?"

"Running. You know…" Cam mimicked jogging in place. "Running from your past. From your wife. From your mom. Even from your own mistakes. What holds you back from forgiving yourself and forgiving your mother? How is any of that any different than you wanting Mallory to forgive you?"

Jonah dropped the box on the floor just outside the door, then sat on the top step. He rested an arm on his knee and dragged a hand over his face. The scent of mildew curled around him.

Cam pressed a hand on his shoulder. "What did you say to me when you pulled into the driveway?"

"'What are we doing here?'" Jonah twisted and looked up at him.

Cam shook his head. "After that."

"Feeling forgetful?"

"Humor me."

"'Mallory and me are through.'"

"Why?"

"Because she doesn't trust me, okay? Do we really need to go through this again? I've tried to prove myself time and time again. I showed up and spent every single day with Tanner, working to build his trust and to bond with him. He's a pretty amazing kid, so that was the easy part. But it still wasn't enough. Not for Mallory. I made a mistake—okay, a big one—and we were back to square one. She overlooked everything I helped her with—learning the farm, supporting her desire to adopt the dogs, pulling the festival together. It wasn't enough, man." Jonah pressed his thumb and fingers against his eyes and lowered his voice. "I wasn't enough. Just like I wasn't enough for Mom to stay."

His throat tightened as his nose burned. To his horror, a tear slid down his cheek, but he wiped away the evidence.

He didn't need to fall apart in front of his cousin. He'd never hear the end of that.

"Jonah."

He stiffened, then sighed. And turned.

Mom stood about a foot behind him, her hands clasped tightly in front of her. "It's time we had that talk."

Jonah braced his elbows on his knees and cradled his head in his hands.

Cam gripped the back of Jonah's neck. "Come on, man. Hear her out. You prayed for her to come home. God listened, even if He took twenty years to answer it."

Knowing his cousin was right, he nodded and pushed to his feet.

It was time to stop running.

Instead of cutting to the garage, Jonah turned and followed her into the living room.

Memories from his childhood swirled around him. Christmas mornings. Opening birthday presents. Watching movies together. The time she took the cushions off the furniture and built a blanket fort and read stories to him after his dog Snickers died.

She stood in front of the window with her back to him.

With her long, red hair pulled back in a loose ponytail, jeans and the light green T-shirt she wore, she looked like a regular mom.

The kind who baked cookies, took him to Scout meetings, attended his baseball games.

But she wasn't a regular mom. She didn't do any of those things.

She'd walked out on him. Somehow, he needed to get past that.

With his arms folded over his chest, he stood in the doorway and waited.

She turned and looked at him with blue eyes that mirrored his. Eyes full of regret. Eyes full of pain. Eyes begging for forgiveness.

Something inside him cracked. His chest shuddered as his throat thickened for the third time that day.

He started to turn away.

"Don't go. Please." The three words, spoken so quietly that he nearly missed them, broke him.

As a tear trailed down his cheek and drifted down his neck, he looked up at her.

She opened her arms.

With two large strides, he crossed the room and walked into her embrace.

As her arms encircled him, something inside his chest broke free, and he released twenty years of pain as he sobbed into her hair like he'd done as a child when life felt unfair.

"I'm sorry. I'm sorry. I'm so sorry," she whispered in his ear.

He nodded, but he couldn't bring himself to break free of her hold.

Cam was right—he'd prayed for years for his mother to come home, and now she was back. He had a choice—to accept her apology or allow the anger and resentment to destroy him bit by bit.

Jonah blew out a breath, ruffling her hair, and pulled back. He rubbed the heel of his hand against his eyes and ran his fingers down his cheeks.

Moving his hands to Mom's shoulders, he looked at her. "I love you, Mom."

Her eyes filled again, and tears spilled down her face. She flung her arms around his neck and pulled him back to her.

His lower back burned, and he sucked in a sharp breath. He untangled himself and rubbed the ache.

"You okay?" The concern in her voice nearly had him rushing back into her arms, as if she could make everything better like she did when he was a kid.

But a blanket fort couldn't fix this.

He nodded, but pivoted and dropped into Dad's dark brown recliner. He rested his head against the cushioned back and released a breath. "Flare-up from my military injuries."

Mom perched on the edge of the matching recliner and reached for his hand. "Your dad told me. I'm so sorry. For so many things."

Jonah squeezed her fingers, then leaned forward and brushed his lips across her knuckles. "I forgive you, Mom. For everything."

Her eyes widened, then she lowered her chin and shook her head. "How can you forgive me after what I've done to you? To your father. I don't deserve it."

He tipped up her chin. "Because God's forgiven me."

She sucked in her bottom lip and struggled with her emotions.

He pushed to his feet and shoved his hands in his front pockets. "We don't deserve God's forgiveness, but He offers it so freely. If He can forgive me, and if I expect Mallory to forgive me, then the least I can do is forgive you. I've had to learn forgiveness is a choice, and I need to do it for my own peace of mind. Otherwise, it feeds the pain and resentment I've been carrying around for twenty years."

She stood and opened her arms once again.

He walked back into them, feeling lighter than he had a few minutes ago.

Mom pulled back and pressed a hand to his cheek. "I love you, Jonah. You are enough. I didn't leave because of you. I had to leave because of me."

"Dad said you were sick, but I didn't know any of that."

"I tried to hide it as much as I could. I struggled with depression. There were days I could barely get out of bed. Finally, I decided you and your dad were better off without me."

"That's not true, Mom."

"I know that now. But I was lost. And oh so broken. But the Lord led me home. Back to you. And your father. For good. With your blessing, I'd love to meet Mallory and get to know my grandson."

"Tanner's a great kid, and you'll love him. Everybody does. Mal's done a great job as a mother. She and I... Well, that's a different story."

Mom grabbed his arm. "Do you love her?"

"With all my heart."

"Then fight for her."

"And if she doesn't want me?"

"Fight harder. You're a marine. You don't back down from a fight. Show her what you're made of, what you two can have together."

He slammed his legs together, stiffened his spine, dropped his left arm at his side, and snapped a salute as if greeting a four-star general. "Aye, aye, ma'am."

"You two about done goofing off in here? We have a basement to clean out." Cam leaned against the doorjamb, hands tucked under his arms and grinning like an idiot.

"Sorry, bro. You're on your own. I need to save my marriage."

Cam moved aside. "It's about time. But you won't have to go far."

Jonah stopped short. "What are you talking about?"

"Mal's here. That's really what I came to tell you."

Jonah's heart stumbled against his ribs. Had he heard correctly? "She's here?"

Cam rolled his eyes and shook his head. "See, I told you that loud music was going to affect your hearing one day."

Jonah glanced back at Mom. "Go, get your girl. I'm not going anywhere. I promise."

For the first time in twenty years, Jonah could rest on that promise.

Chapter Fifteen

Maybe she should've called first.

It was kind of late. What if Jonah rejected her? He'd seemed pretty upset when he left the farm earlier that afternoon.

But she refused to allow her fears to get in the way of her future.

Not anymore.

With the moon full overhead, she sat on the old swing that hung from the giant oak in Leland's backyard.

She gripped the aged rope as she twisted herself on the swing. As she released her foothold on the ground and allowed the swing to twirl her in the opposite direction, the back door opened, spilling light into the yard illuminated by the stars.

Jonah's broad frame filled the doorway as he scanned the yard. Then he stepped off the back deck and headed in her direction.

She stood and pressed a hand to her stomach.

This was it. The deciding factor in what the future would hold for them.

Mallory started across the yard and met him halfway. Even though his face was shadowed, she didn't miss the tightness in his jaw.

That did little to settle the churning in her stomach.

"Hi." She gave him a little wave, then jerked a thumb over her shoulder. "Nice swing."

Then she cringed. Seriously? That was the best she had to offer?

"Dad and I made it when I was about Tanner's age. I thought it was lame in high school, but he refused to take it down. So it stayed, getting beat up by the elements."

She clasped her hands in front of her and rubbed her thumb along her fingers. "Kind of like us."

"What do you want, Mallory?" Hands on his hips, he leveled her with a no-nonsense look.

Pressure built behind her eyes as his words bounced around in her head. Without taking time to overthink what her heart longed to speak, she pulled in a lungful of air and released it slowly. Then she reached into the front pocket of her jeans and retrieved her wedding band. Her fingers tightened around it for a moment, then she held it up to him. "You. I want you."

Just saying the words filled her with more courage than she'd felt in a very long time. She steeled her spine and allowed her eyes to rove over his face, his hair.

"You are a man of integrity, and you've made me feel more secure than I have in a very long time. I'm sorry for what I said and not trusting you completely. I allowed my fears to get the best of me. I want to say it won't happen again, but I can't. I've come to realize my brain is wired differently, but I don't want to allow my anxiety to come between us."

He remained quiet, studying her.

"You were as scared as I was looking for Tanner. The reason I know he likes to wander is because I lost him once in the grocery store. The most terrifying ten minutes until I found him sitting on the floor in the cereal aisle." She shifted on her feet and started to pocket the ring.

His hand shot forward and caught hers. "Don't."

"Don't what?"

"Don't put it away."

He opened her hand and took the ring off her palm. He slipped it into his pocket. Then his fingers trailed up her arm, over her shoulder and around her neck as he bridged the distance between them.

Her chest pinched as the courage she'd mustered earlier drained from her. He'd taken away the one thing that had been a symbol of hope for her. Hope for their marriage. Hope for their family. Hope for their future together.

Head bent, she tried to brush past him, but he caught her arm. "Where are you going?"

She lifted her hands, then dropped them and shook her head. "I don't know. You pocketed my ring, and now I feel..."

Her turned her around and cradled her face in his hands. "You feel what?"

She tried to shrug, but he was so close. Her shoulders rubbed against his. "Lost."

"You're not lost, Mal. You're right here. With me. Where you belong."

She searched his face. His jaw relaxed, and the tiny lines in the corners of his eyes deepened. But it was the tenderness of his touch that gave her what she needed now more than anything.

Hope. And his love.

She slipped her hands over his chest then slid her arms around his neck. "I love you, Jonah. Even when I hated you for what you'd done to me, to Tanner, and never wanted to see you again, I still loved you. I want our marriage to be real in every way. Tanner needs his father, and we need to be a family together."

Jonah's hands rested at her waist. "I love you, too, Mallory. I want nothing more than for us to have a real marriage and be a family together. For Tanner's sake and for ours. You're strong and independent. And a little stubborn."

She laughed softly and raised an eyebrow. "And you're not?"

He chuckled too. "Lord, help us. For Tanner's sake…and any other children we have."

She stifled a squeal. "You want more kids?"

"I grew up as an only child. While it has its perks, it does get lonely at times."

"I love my siblings, but I will say, I would've given up my brothers in a heartbeat when we were growing up. They wouldn't leave me alone."

"And now they're your biggest protectors. After me, of course."

"Are you sure you want to do this? I am stubborn and independent."

"And strong. But we are stronger together."

"*Together.* I love the sound of that."

He shot her one of those grins that caused her heart to cartwheel and picked her up and spun her around. As soon as her feet touched the grass, he lowered his mouth and covered hers.

Jonah released her, reached into his pocket and pulled out her ring. "More than anything, I want to put this on your finger this very second and claim you as my wife."

"What's stopping you?"

Was she ready for his answer?

"We have a lot to discuss. Important decisions to make." He entwined her fingers within his and pulled her close to him once again. "I want to do this right. And I want you to be sure."

"I'm sure. Definitely sure. In fact, first thing Monday morning, I'm making an appointment with the DMV to get my name changed on my driver's license to match the one on my marriage certificate."

He smiled. "While I love the sound of that, what if you wait?"

She froze. "Wait? You want me to wait?"

Jonah tightened his arms around her. Her cheek rested against his chest, and she listened to the steady beating of his heart.

She'd told him she loved him and trusted him. So why wouldn't he want her to change her name?

Maybe it was her turn to prove herself to him. Whatever it was, she'd do it because she didn't want them to be apart again.

Jonah hadn't expected his question to be met with silence.

"What's going on inside that beautiful head of yours?"

She shrugged, the material of her shirt rustling against his T-shirt.

He loosened his hold but didn't release her and tipped up her chin. "What's wrong?"

Mallory stepped out of his arms and turned her back to him. "Why do you want me to wait to change my driver's license?"

Ah, that.

Of course.

He should've known his response would spark her insecurities.

"Because like I said—I want to do it right this time. Mallory?"

She turned. Then her eyes widened at finding him on one knee and holding her ring between his thumb and forefinger. Her hands flew to her mouth. "Jonah!"

"I fell in love with you when we reconnected at the NCO club. When we said our vows, I'd expected to keep them. But then I allowed stupidity to cloud my thinking, and I made the biggest mistake of my life. I want to make things right with a fresh start. Mallory Stone Hayes, will you do me the honor of renewing our wedding vows and making a new life with me? I love you, and I promise to protect your heart for the rest of our lives."

Nodding, she lowered herself to her knees in front of him and took his hands between hers. "Yes. Even though I loved our tiny beach wedding, I think a fresh start with our family and friends present is exactly what we need to put the past to rest. I promise to trust you with my whole heart, and look forward to expanding our family with you."

"Um, I never did get you an engagement ring."

"I don't need one." She curled his fingers over her wedding band. "You hold on to this until you can put it on my finger for good. Then it's never coming off."

He kissed her again and slid his arms around her waist. "So when can we do this vow renewal? Is tomorrow too soon?"

She laughed. "Yes, I think so. Let's talk to Cam and Bri about the farm and then hold it there."

He stood and pulled her up with him. "Do you want to stay?"

"Only if you're willing to remain with me. Stronger together, remember?"

"I'll always be by your side."

"That's the perfect place to be." She shivered.

He wrapped an arm around her and guided her to the back door. "Let's head inside and share the good news. Plus, I want you to meet my mom."

Jonah opened the back door and ushered her inside. He took a moment for his eyes to adjust to the sudden brightness. Then he took Mallory's hand and followed the voices to the living room.

Dad sat in his favorite recliner while his uncle sat in the matching one. Cam and Bri snuggled next to each other on the couch while Mom sat opposite them on the love seat with her bare feet tucked under her. She never did like wearing shoes.

When he and Mallory appeared in the doorway, talking stopped and all eyes trained on them.

Holding Mallory's hand tightly, he looked at his family. "So, we have some news."

Dad lowered the footrest on his recliner and sat up. "What's going on?"

Jonah looked at Mallory and dropped a kiss on the tip of her nose. "Mallory has agreed to be my wife...again. We want to renew our vows in front of our family and friends."

Bri clapped her hands and squealed. She bounced off and rushed over to Mallory. She flung her arms around both of them. "I'm so happy for you guys."

Cam joined them and pulled Bri to his side. "So, Bri and I have been talking."

She pressed her clasped hands to her mouth and bounced on the balls of her feet. "We want you to have the farm."

Cam laughed. "Thanks for letting me take charge of the conversation, babe."

Bri rested her head on Cam's shoulder. "Sorry. I guess I got carried away."

Jonah frowned and looked at his cousin. "What are you two talking about, man?"

"Just like I said—we want you to have the farm. We've seen what you've done over the past couple of months and feel you're the best ones to take it over."

Pulling Mallory close, Jonah smiled down at her. "Of course we are. Stronger together, right?"

She cupped his cheek. "Always."

Jonah dragged his attention away from his wife and refocused on Cam. "Now that we have our relationship squared away, we're definitely getting the farm. Once we do the finances at the bank, we'll get you a check."

Cam held up two hands. "No, man, you misunderstood. We want you to have the farm. No loan. No mortgage. 'Have' as in a gift."

Jonah's lungs deflated. He opened his mouth, but words refused to come out.

Mallory tightened her hold on his hand. "Why would you give us the farm?"

Her breathy words held a mix of emotion and disbelief.

Bri reached for her other hand. "You've always been like a sister to me. I talked to my parents, and they agreed—there's no one else we'd like to see have it. Cam and I wanted to give it to you all along, but you're both so stubborn so we came up with the idea of having you partner together."

"Oh, you did, did you?" Jonah slugged Cam playfully in the shoulder, then grabbed him in a hug. "Thanks, man. I don't know what to say."

"Dude, you just did—thanks is enough. Oh, yeah, invite us to the vow renewal."

Jonah looked down at Mallory. Not taking his eyes off her, he said, "Keep next weekend open because we don't want to wait any longer than we have to."

Not caring who was watching, he lowered his mouth once again and kissed his wife.

Epilogue

Mallory didn't know why she'd kept the dress in the back of her closet. From moving to different duty stations to being deployed, she'd purged so much. But the white sundress—with its sweetheart neckline, flounced hem and spaghetti straps that tied at the shoulders—remained among the things she didn't have the heart to give away.

While she was thankful for remaining sentimental and keeping the dress she'd worn when she and Jonah exchanged their vows, it was time for a fresh start.

And that meant a new dress. One she'd chosen with her mother and sisters present this time.

She smoothed a hand over the champagne-colored sleeveless gown with a beaded bodice and embroidered overlay. With her hair in loose curls down her back and a gold pendant of a tulip—a gift from Jonah and Tanner—Mallory was ready to become Mrs. Jonah Hayes once again.

She gathered her hand-tied bouquet of multi-colored tulips—Miss Mari's artwork—and left her room. With a hand on the banister, she took her time descending the stairs, careful not to catch her heel on the carpet.

Jonah waited for her at the bottom of the stairs. Dressed in a white untucked button-down shirt and tan pants, he looked even more handsome than he had eight years ago.

As she approached, his eyes darkened. He took her hand and helped her with the last step. Then he leaned in close, his mouth brushing her ear. "You look incredible."

"Thank you." She pressed a hand over her fluttering stomach. "You look pretty great yourself."

He extended his elbow. "Ready?"

"Absolutely." She placed her hand in the crook of his arm and allowed him to lead her out the front door.

As they moved down the farmhouse steps, soft music drifted across the yard and guided them to the orchard, where Pastor Miles stood under the sprawling branches of apple trees ripe with budding fruit.

Jonah had constructed a wooden arch that Mom, Macey, Piper, Callie and Everly had draped with white fabric, greenery, and tulips in yellow, red and white.

As they stopped in front of the arch, Tanner, dressed like his dad, ran over to them and stood between them, taking each of their hands.

Their families gathered in a semicircle around them. As Mallory gazed around at those who loved them most, she couldn't stop the welling of tears that threatened to spill down her face.

They were blessed. Truly blessed.

"Family, friends, we gather together to celebrate and reaffirm the union between Jonah Leland and Mallory Erin. They have come together to make a fresh start and renew the vows of love, honor and commitment they spoke eight years ago. Mallory and Jonah have chosen to share their own vows with one another." Pastor Miles looked at Mallory and gave her a slight nod.

She handed her bouquet to Tanner and took both of Jonah's hands. "Jonah, I said this before and I mean it with my whole heart. You are a man of integrity and intention. You've earned my trust in so many different ways. Thank you for loving me, for supporting my dreams and helping me to become a better person. You are an amazing father, and I look forward to growing old with you." A tear drifted down her cheek as she looked at him with all the love in her heart. She slid his wedding band back on his finger, where it belonged.

Gently, he wiped away her tear and took her left hand. He placed the simple gold band on her finger that fit so well and then brushed his lips across her knuckles as if to seal it into place.

"Mallory, thank you for trusting me, believing in me and for giving me many new opportunities to show you how much I love you. As we journey through our adventures together, there's no one I'd rather have by my side but you."

"Hey, what about me?" Tanner piped up, causing a low rumble of laughter to ripple through their gathered family and friends.

Jonah wrapped an arm around Tanner's shoulders and moved him between them. He took Mallory's hand and kept one on their son. "Allow me to amend my previous statement. There's no one I'd rather have by my side but the two of you."

Tanner looked up at Jonah with such adoration that Mallory couldn't stop the tears if she tried. A glance at her family showed she wasn't the only one with wet eyes. She returned her focus to the man she loved with her whole heart.

Jonah gave her hand a gentle squeeze. "Stronger together."

Pastor Miles reaffirmed them as husband and wife and invited Jonah to kiss his bride.

Jonah edged Tanner out of the way. "Sorry, buddy. Now it's my turn."

He swept his fingers around her neck and pulled her close. She rested her hand on his shoulder as his lips brushed hers. "I love you, Mal."

"I love you, too, Jonah. Always and forever."

The midafternoon sunshine warmed her shoulders as a gentle breeze rustled through the trees, stirring the leaves. Birds serenaded them from the branches as Jonah gathered her in his arms, and there wasn't any other place that she'd rather be.

* * * * *

Dear Reader,

Mallory's love for senior dogs was inspired by a high school friend of mine and her husband, who rescue elderly dogs so they can live out their final years with a loving family.

My own life has changed since becoming a dog mom. Our family has been blessed to receive unconditional love and affection from two beauties who have since crossed the Rainbow Bridge—Samantha and Penny. Now, we have two rascally rescue dogs—Ollie and Finn, who keep us quite busy.

There's something so uplifting about the love of a dog who doesn't judge you for past mistakes. It's a similar kind of love God has for us. A love that is pure and offers redemption that helps us heal from past mistakes.

By recognizing those inevitable mistakes, we can use them as opportunities to change, and become the men and women God wants us to be. Every stumble can lead to growth and redemption if we are willing to lean into the Lord and trust Him through the painful healing process.

In *Earning the Veteran's Trust*, Mallory and Jonah learned to let go of their fears in order to trust the Lord and one another as they overcame past mistakes. By embracing their faith, they were reminded the Lord wouldn't leave them or forsake them and then able to trust God's plan for their lives.

We were created for relationships—with the Lord and with one another. Stronger together. May you find the same kind of unconditional love as you lean into the Lord and embrace the hope and purpose He has for you.

Embracing His Grace,
Lisa Jordan

Harlequin® Reader Service

Enjoyed your book?

Try the perfect subscription for Romance readers and get more great books like this delivered right to your door.

See why over 10+ million readers have tried Harlequin Reader Service.

Start with a Free Welcome Collection with free books and a gift—valued over $20.

Choose any series in print or ebook. See website for details and order today:

TryReaderService.com/subscriptions